# Ghosts
# of
# North Texas

## Mitchel Whitington

**Republic of Texas Press**
**Plano, Texas**

**Library of Congress Cataloging-in-Publication Data**

Whitington, Mitchel.
   Ghosts of north Texas / Mitchel Whitington.
     p.  cm.
   ISBN  1-55622-940-2 (alk. paper)
   1. Ghosts--Texas.  2. Haunted places--Texas.  I. Title.
   BF1472.U6 W49   2004
   133.1'09764--dc21                   2002010847
                                      CIP

Republic of Texas Press is an imprint of Wordware Publishing, Inc.
No part of this book may be reproduced in any form or by
any means without permission in writing from
Wordware Publishing, Inc.

Printed in the United States of America

Photos by author except where otherwise noted.

ISBN 1-55622-940-2
10 9 8 7 6 5 4 3 2 1
0107

All inquiries for volume purchases of this book should be addressed to
Wordware Publishing, Inc., at 2320 Los Rios Boulevard, Plano, Texas
75074. Telephone inquiries may be made by calling:
(972) 423-0090

For my parents, Leonard and Betty Whitington,
who have given me a lifetime of love and support;

For Denise Vitola,
a dear friend to whom I owe undying thanks
for my writing career;

For the spirits of The Grove, whoever they may be,
that continue to inspire me;

And for my wife, Tami,
for believing.

# Contents

*Contents*

# A Preface

Chrome. Glass. Steel. An ultra-modern world, with one suburb blending seamlessly into the next. The spirit realm might seem dimensions away from places in North Texas such as the Dallas/Fort Worth Metroplex—and rightfully so. Interstate highways loop around onto themselves, forming a never-ending snake of traffic. Chain restaurants have exploded onto every major intersection, and any modern convenience is only a short drive away.

It sounds like a very unlikely location to find ghosts...but don't be too hasty. North Texas is actually steeped in history, from the old cattle paths of Fort Worth, to the Preston trail that took immigrant and freighter traffic through the early settlement of Dallas. Plantations and farms covered the surrounding countryside with blood and sweat, and the network of railroads brought in their own flavor of adventure and notoriety.

The suburbs and small towns that dot the North Texas area have adventurous stories of their own and are the locations for some of the most interesting haunted places in the state.

As the modern world expanded over these sites of trouble and turmoil, new buildings inherited old spirits, and the legacy of hauntings began. Ghosts have appeared in some of the most improbable of places, making this section of North Texas one of the most haunted areas of the state.

Come explore these mysterious sites, and meet some of their inhabitants: the spirit of an eighty-year-old woman who simply won't accept the fact that she's dead; a ghostly man intent on protecting women traveling alone to a beautiful bed and breakfast; a restaurant where phantom voices and footsteps haunt the staff and patrons, and many, many more. They are all waiting for you, should you dare to explore the haunted side of North Texas!

## So what are these things called ghosts?

What are ghosts? To be honest, I wish I knew. I've seen them, felt them, heard them—even smelled them, but I couldn't begin to tell you what they are.

Some folks will let you know straight out that the earth-bound spirits are the souls of those who have died but for some reason just haven't moved on to their next destination yet.

Other people swear they are demons, sent by the Devil himself to trick unsuspecting humans for some diabolical purpose.

There are those who subscribe to the theory put forth by physicist Steven Hawking that time is not linear but instead is like a river with little swirls and eddies that often flow back onto themselves. If this is true, then perhaps the things that we perceive as ghosts are really pieces of the past or future bleeding over into our present.

Yet another theory is that they are merely energy patterns left behind after some emotionally charged moment that occurred years ago, just like you'll continue to see the image of a camera's flash long after it goes off when someone takes your picture.

Me? I simply don't know. A friend of mine explained to me one time that he keeps a "mental drawer" where he stores things that he doesn't understand, and that's kind of the way I am when it comes to ghosts. With every new experience, every scrap of information, I open that little mental drawer up in my head and file it away. Occasionally I even go through all the contents, just to see if any of it fits together or makes any sense. Sometimes things do, sometimes things don't. Like Michelangelo said on the occasion of his eighty-seventh birthday, however, *"Ancoro imparo"*—"I am still learning." Until I do understand these specters, or perhaps become one myself, I intend to continue to try to learn about these spirits that walk among us. And in the pages of this book, I'd like to invite you to *join me.*

# The places we'll be visiting

This book is a travel guide to haunted locations in North Texas. Many are restaurants, inns, and other buildings that have tenants who experience the supernatural on a regular basis. You'll find stories from these people that I've interviewed, notes on my own impressions of these places, along with information on how to go take a look for yourself.

Other sites that I've included are those that are rumored to be haunted, but no witnesses to any paranormal activity exist. These are in the book for informational purposes, and because—let's face it—it's always fun to tell ghost stories!

Finally, there are a few North Texas places that are supposedly haunted, but in reality are simply urban legends—the kind of tales that people love to tell around the campfire. I'd be a terrible host if I didn't stop to point these out along the way.

# A Special Thank-You To

As the author of this ghostly little journey through North Texas, I'd be terribly remiss if I didn't take a second to thank several people who made this book possible. When I've written fiction in the past, it was easy enough to sit back and let the words flow from my own mind. This is a work of nonfiction, however, and includes the stories and eyewitness accounts from many people who were kind enough to spare a little of their time for me. I know there's no way I can put such a list together without missing a few people, though, and so I'll apologize in advance; I really don't want to leave anyone out. All that said, in no certain order I'd like to thank:

Ginnie Bivona, the best editor on the planet, for trusting me to do this book; Charlie LeMay, for taking me along to look for the black Corvette those twenty-odd years ago; Grover McMains from the Texas White House for the tape; Lisa and Jeff for patiently snacking on cheese fries at Snuffer's while I asked the waiter all sorts of questions about the ghosts, and the waiter himself, whose name I never got; Off-Off-Broadway playwright Molly Louise Shepard and Mnemonyss, two strangers connected by the sighting of a dark man (more about Molly at http://members.tripod.com/MollyLou/); Bill Campbell, for a great visit and for hooking me up with the ghost stories; the two police officers eating burgers on Preston Road; Vaughn Franks from the Bonnynook Inn, for letting me just drop in; The former Six Flags employees—see, I told you that I wouldn't use your names; David Davis from the elegant Adolphus Hotel for showing me the place... Wow; Richard Rey from lifeadventures.com, for letting me quote and for one heckuva great travel magazine; Dwight and Sheila Greene from Greene's Antiques, and Dwight's delightful mother for the tour; Lois Reed, from *The Dallas Morning News* for helping me resolve the quote permission questions; Lonnie Allen from the Stockyards Hotel for the info; Steven Barnett, drummer for the band Baboon (http://www.baboonland.com/)—it took a lot of nerve to lock yourself in the attic with the ghost; Joanna San Angelo, director of the Sammons Center for the Arts, for a wealth of information and letting me see your incredible building; Louis Brown from the Chaska House, for the patience while we tried to hook up; Andy Grieser, reporter and ghost hunter, for laying tracks that I'd later use in this book; the chef at Del Frisco's Double Eagle, although he didn't contribute anything to the book, MAN what a steak; Jake Jegelewicz, former Olla Podrida merchant—great bike, dude; Vicki Bayliff for setting the record straight about Screaming Bridge, and Michael Bayliff for showing me the site; Pat Lovelace from the Tarlton House Bed and Breakfast, especially for a wonderful visit on the front porch; the bartender at the Sons of Hermann Hall, for telling me stories and pouring me a cold one—uh, make that two; Robin Fletcher, tour guide at the Baker Hotel, I appreciate the information; Evelyn Williams from the Baroness Inn, the most delightful person on the planet; Joe Peters Sr. from Peters Brothers Hats, a man who is truly blessed; Joan Upton Hall and Stacey Hasbrook, for their information on the Granbury Opera House; Sheila Walker, for her wonderful Jett stories; Vicki Isaacs, co-founder of Metroplex Paranormal Investigations (visit them at metroplexparanormalinvestigations.com); Jack, from the Jack-in-the-Box Corporation, because I pretty much used their clean restrooms exclusively during my travels around North Texas researching this book...oh, and for Sourdough Jacks —those sustained me on the road; Brandon, for being willing to give me an interview, even though we didn't actually hook up; Chris and Angie Baker, for relaying the stories to me; Jimmy Poarch, for the intriguing stories and several years of delicious catfish; Louis Brown, for allowing me to use his wonderful B&B in this book; WAY TOO MANY librarians and historians across North Texas to name—thanks for all your help; and Peggye, for sharing her own beliefs about life after death as I was writing this book, and giving me interesting things to contemplate....

# A Few Words on Ghost Hunting

I sincerely hope that you'll visit some of the places in this book, just to see for yourself what might be going on there. There are a few basic items of ghost-hunting etiquette to cover before we get started, though.

1) Always be safe and legal. Don't trespass or cross any boundaries that you aren't supposed to, and don't take any chances with your safety. If you decide to explore an old cemetery at midnight, chances are any passing officer of the law will stop to ask you a few questions, or a criminal might seize the opportunity to take your wallet. Know the rules concerning any place that you visit.

2) Respect other people's property. If you are visiting a haunted restaurant, it would be rude to head directly into the kitchen with your video camera rolling tape. It's much more fun to strike up a conversation with a waiter and let him tell you where some of the ghosts have been seen.

3) Ask what kind of supernatural activity has been occurring lately and where it has been located. When I get ready to visit a bed & breakfast that has a spirit or two, I always inquire in advance about which rooms have been the most active, and then I try to get a reservation in one of those rooms for the evening.

4) Plan to put in a little time. Unfortunately, ghosts seem to show up on their own schedule, not ours. I've had experiences on the first night of staying in a bed & breakfast, but then again, I've dined in a particular haunted restaurant dozens of times without a single chill running down my spine. Realize that you're simply not going to have an experience every time you go out, and enjoy them when they do occur.

5) When you are having a paranormal experience, try not to be afraid. Believe me, that's much easier said than done! You have to change your way of thinking about ghosts, though.

Forget about every horror movie you've ever seen. They're rubbish and nonsense—albeit *entertaining* rubbish and nonsense. A Hollywood ghost story is to a real haunting what John Wayne's *The Alamo* is to the real story of that mission in San Antonio. I've never had an experience where I felt threatened by a ghost—only my own fears!

6) Know what an experience with a ghost is. It may be the sudden, strong odor of cigar smoke that makes its way down the hallway of a non-smoking restaurant. It could also be a sudden drop in temperature around you, or something much less tangible, such as the feeling that you are not alone in a room. In a haunted bookstore in Fort Worth, the sound of pages turning can be heard upstairs when the building is closed and there are no patrons left inside. The most rare experience of all is actually seeing the full form of a ghost, although it does happen. At a bed & breakfast in Milford, the ghost of a lady actually entered one of the bedrooms and conversed with the couple staying there.

## Believing in ghosts

Sometimes people tell me, "I don't believe in ghosts." I usually just smile and answer, "What makes you think that they believe in you?"

There are far too many recorded experiences with ghosts from people of every walk of life to dismiss their presence. If a person is interested in finding a ghost, it is easy enough to do, so the idea of "not believing in ghosts" is like saying, "the Great Wall of China isn't there," simply because you haven't seen it for yourself. While we may not know definitively what they are, the fact remains, something does exist.

Many people are afraid to believe in ghosts, though, because they won't let themselves even try to understand them. To study ghosts is to actually allow your mind to cross the threshold of death and nose around a little bit. Few people can do that without contemplating their own mortality, which is probably the deepest fear inside of us all.

To my mind, ghosts aren't a reminder that I'm going to die someday. They are instead an indication that there is something beyond the few years we get to spend on Earth, and that perhaps there are things more important than the trinkets and dramas that we find ourselves caught up in every day.

But don't decide right now whether or not you will allow yourself to accept the idea of ghosts; we have many places to visit. Come along with me, and experience the spirits of North Texas for yourself!

# The Ghosts of Arlington

*A*h, Arlington, a place that I remember as a kid's paradise, and the perfect way to begin our ghostly little journey through North Texas. As I first started my research, I found more ghost stories about Arlington, per capita, than any other city in North Texas. They had colorful names such as "Legacy Park," "Hell's Gate," "The Hobo," "Screaming Bridge," "Crystal Canyon," and many more.

I'd heard that Arlington was a historic old town, so my first thought was perhaps the spirited activity that was rumored to be there came naturally. I was looking forward to checking it out, because I have many fond memories of Arlington from my childhood. After all, it held the magical world of Six Flags, along with other places such as the Wax Museum. But this was long before Ripley's Believe it or Not, the Ballpark, or any of the water parks that line Interstate 30 now. When it came right down to it, I guess, all I really knew about the town was what I could see from the Six Flags Oil Derrick.

As I started combing the city for haunted locations, I found out that it has a background I'd never dreamed of. Arlington was started all the way back in 1876. The soil was perfect for the farmers to grow fruits and vegetables, from the fertile black land to the sandy loam, and there seemed to be an endless supply of water from the Trinity River and its tributaries.

Things were tough for the people there, though—Indian attacks happened quite frequently, until a treaty was signed between the settlers and the natives. Once the threat of attack had subsided, the community began to grow in earnest, boasting several cotton gins to process the farmers' main crop. Farmers in the

1

Arlington area also grew grains such as oats and hay, and produce like corn, peanuts, potatoes, and more.

Something I had never heard about was a town moneymaker for several years in Arlington—a fountain that gave healing water! A public well had been dug, and it turned out that the well produced mineral water. When the craze of healing water hit, the liquid was bottled and sold to the people visiting the town. So many folks were coming through the city to get the miracle cure that a resort was built for them, a sanitarium where they could relax and take the mineral water treatment.

The town grew steadily, with additions such as colleges, a General Motors assembly plant, and eventually the sports and entertainment parks that have made it famous today.

All very interesting, but I wanted to find out about the ghost stories that were in the city. When I actually got down to doing a little digging, I found that many were just spooky campfire tales—"tales of the hook" type things. There were a few that were very interesting, though, and I even included the truth about "Screaming Bridge" in this section, although it turned out that there weren't any spirits there.

Ready? Then let's take a look at the haunted side of Arlington: a historic fort that was one of the earliest settlements there, a legendary buried treasure and the ghosts who supposedly guard it, the real story behind "Screaming Bridge," and even a stop at Six Flags Over Texas!

## Annie and the Kandy Kitchen

Thank God for Angus G. Wynne Jr.—he was truly a great man. I'm honestly surprised that more statures haven't been erected to this wondrous gentleman. You see, that fellow had a vision that was realized on August 5, 1961, when he opened the gates of a wonderful, magical land to the rest of the world. During its inception, several names were tossed around for the park, including "The Great Southwest" and "Texas Under Six Flags." When the main entrance swung open that glorious day, however, the name was a decisive SIX FLAGS OVER TEXAS!

You'd be hard pressed to find an adult in North Texas who didn't go to Six Flags as a teenager, whether on a family vacation, a Senior day, or a church youth group trip. I certainly remember my experiences at Six Flags: eating the delicious Pink Things that are sold in the park, sitting through those wonderfully air-conditioned shows at the Southern Palace on hot summer days, and shopping at The Spectrum, that cube-shaped store with all the black light posters. At the time, the fastest ride in the park was the Runaway Mine Train, and the big drop on the coaster was right after the cars went into the western saloon. What a blast that was. And of course, my now-wife and I stood in line over and over at The Cave, to drift along the river in the dark, watch those glowing stalactite-headed spelunkers, and make out like crazy for the entire course of the ride.

Those were the days. But apparently something else was going on in the park that few people knew about—a spirited visitor to the Kandy Kitchen building in the Texas section, one of the original shops that opened with the park in 1961. To this day it is still a wonderful place with delicious scents wafting though its doors, where you can purchase fudge, caramel apples, and many varieties of scrumptious candies. Finding the ghost there, however, is a rare occurrence.

Normally, when you encounter a ghost it is when the setting is quiet and still so that your senses can focus solely on that one experience. Six Flags Over Texas is anything but quiet, which may be the very reason more people don't know about the ghost. I've known about the stories of the haunted Kandy Kitchen for some time, with the spirit of the little girl there who is sometimes called Annie, sometimes Amy. As to whether or not she really exists, I have to say I personally never sensed the spirit that lurks around the yellow candy store. But how would one notice? At any given time your blood is pounding from the last thrill ride, the excitement and energy around you is at a peak, you're drenched from one of the water rides, and the chance to simply stop and peacefully soak in the surroundings is rare. Six Flags is just too much fun for that.

Long past the days of Mr. Wynne, the park has become a cog in a huge corporation, and since mega-corporations and ghosts usually don't mix, I wanted to talk to someone who had experienced the spirit for himself. I was on a mission to uncover any details about the candy store ghost. It stood to reason that if anyone had experienced the phantom, it would have to be the people who were there in the lonely hours before the park opened or after it had closed for the evening. I knew that to fully explore the possibility, I had to tap into the folks who worked the store and the food services crowd.

Fortunately for me, the former employees of Six Flags Over Texas have an organization for exchanging addresses and information, and I was able to stir up a few people who had worked at the Kandy Kitchen at one time or another. They all knew about the ghost, and a few didn't want to talk about it at all. Three good folks were kind enough to let me ask a few questions, but they would only let me quote them anonymously—not that they were afraid of repercussions from the park, but out of respect that it is more employee lore, not an official part of the Six Flags. No problem. They were enjoyable to talk with and sincere in their stories.

One of the three laughed out loud when I first asked about the ghost. She worked at Six Flags in the mid-1980s, and one of her assignments was the candy store in the Texas section. "We called the ghost Annie, and she was just one of those things that we joked about," the former employee said, "especially when a new kid got assigned to the shop. We'd fill them full of stories about the ghost then send them upstairs to get some stock. They'd always come running back down the stairs! I don't think there was really a ghost in the building, though. It was simply something for the old-timers, as we liked to call ourselves, to use on the new guys."

The second person wasn't as cavalier, though. "At any given time there was a couple of us working the shop, and we'd occasionally hear what sounded like footsteps on the storage floor above us. No one was up there, of course, but we got to the point where we'd just smile and say, 'Hi Annie!' That was the name that everyone in Food Services knew her by. Every now and then someone would claim to have seen her up on the faux balcony or in the upstairs window, but I never actually saw anything."

My final contact from Six Flags' bygone days had the most interesting story, though. "We didn't have the only ghost in the park," she said. "The folks over at the Southern Palace claimed they had a ghost, but every actor says that about their theater. We really had one at Texas Kandy. The story I'd heard was that a young girl drowned in a creek years ago before Six Flags started construction, and the Texas Kandy shop is built over the site. Annie is attracted to the candy store, as any young girl would be, and since she seems to be so friendly we put up with her antics and pranks. Nothing major—turning lights off occasionally, knocking something over, just little things to let us know she was there."

So what is true? Well, it's hard to say. On October 25, 1996, a spokesman for the park, Keith Salwoski, told the *Arlington Morning News*, "People in our park swear to have seen the ghost in the building."

The stories go on about a young girl named Annie being kidnapped back in the 1920s when the area was home to the Arlington

Downs Racetrack. The tale varies, depending on the person telling it, but the commonality is that the little girl was murdered,
drowned in a nearby creek, etc. However the workers at the candy
store report nothing but a benevolent spirit that occasionally
shows up.

I guess the bottom line is this: If you visit Six Flags Over
Texas, ride all the thrill rides, hit the latest coasters, go up in the
oil derrick, and take in a show or two. You're going to have a wonderful time. While you're visiting the park, though, stop by the
two-story yellow building in the Texas section of the park and ask
the people there about the ghost. Chances are, Annie may have
drifted through there recently.

Six Flags Over Texas
2201 Road to Six Flags
Arlington, TX 76010
Phone: 817.530.6000
Web: http://www.sixflags.com/parks/overtexas/home.asp

# The Screaming Bridge
# to Mosier Valley

When I first heard about a place named "Screaming Bridge," I
immediately dismissed it as another fanciful tale. I could only
imagine that it was one of those stories where there was a ficti-
tious car wreck at some time in the past, and if you stop your car
and honk your horn on the bridge at midnight, or some other
magic time, you can hear the scream of the driver.

The name of the place just kept coming up, though, so I
decided to do a little digging just to see what was there. As it turns
out, the story of Screaming Bridge is a tragic one, and the events
were very real: racial hatred, a horrible car wreck, and many lives
shattered.

To begin with, the name "Screaming Bridge" was given to a
small, one-lane bridge that crossed the Trinity River on old

Looking out across the former site of Screaming Bridge

Harrison Road (now known as Davis). Its name came from the fact that the bridge was so old that when a car crossed, the timbers would creak and moan, as if it were screaming from the strain of the weight. Vicki Bayliff, a resident of Arlington who grew up not far from the bridge, told me, "It was just a thrill ride over a very old bridge. I was always wondering if it was going to collapse while driving over it. It never did, of course; it just sounded really spooky."

On the other side of the bridge was an area of town known as Mosier Valley. The community was established in the 1870s by emancipated slave families, most of whom were freed from the Mosier plantation. The Trinity River bottomland was given to the freedmen by the Mosier family, and the African Americans established a close-knit farming community there. To get to Mosier Valley from Arlington, one would first cross Screaming Bridge, then a smaller bridge just before a railroad track.

In the 1960s, a very turbulent time in our nation's history, there were individuals who were violently opposed to any integration between races. A few such individuals set fire to the smaller bridge before the railroad track, probably assuming that an accident there would deter any African Americans from coming into Arlington from Mosier Valley. Hate always clouds the mind, though, and what the individuals failed to take into consideration was that many people, regardless of race, frequently crossed the bridge. According to Vicki, "Other than cruising around the Three Pal's, the Bull Pen, and going out to Feather Beach and the main beach at Arlington, driving out north of town down the dark country roads and crossing over the Screaming Bridge was pretty much all there was to do."

The railroad discovered that the bridge had been burned out and posted warning signs on both sides. Someone removed those signs, however, so that there would be no notification to drivers that the bridge was out. On an evening in February of 1961, a car full of teenaged girls was out cruising after seeing a drive-in movie in Fort Worth—three girls in the front seat, three in the back. Vicki remembers the accident well, since she attended Arlington High School with the young people involved. "The kids had gone over the Screaming Bridge and were headed towards the railroad crossing. The girls did not know that the smaller bridge was out until they got right on top of it. The driver tried to gun the motor to jump over the bridge onto the railroad tracks. They did not make it, and they drove head-on into the embankment on the other side. The three girls in the front seat died. One of the girls' fathers was an Arlington cop and was sent to investigate the accident, and he had no idea that he would be the one to find his daughter dead. It was a horrible thing to happen. The three in the back seat were injured but survived the wreck."

It was a tragedy for everyone involved. The perpetrators of the bridge burning finally stepped forward and took responsibility for the death of the girls. They were three senior boys from Arlington High School, along with another young friend, and they were expelled from school and not allowed to graduate. A reward was posted for the people who removed the signs, but they were never identified.

There are many legends that are floating around about Screaming Bridge, and most start with the idea that the wreck occurred on the bridge and involved two cars. From there, some of the tales are:

✧ If you stand on the bridge and look down into the water, the date of the accident and the names of the girls who died will be on glowing tombstones in the river.

✧ Sit in the middle of the bridge on the anniversary of the night of the accident, and at midnight a heavy fog will rise up from the river and you will see headlights approaching the bridge.

✧ Go to the bridge on the accident's anniversary at midnight, and the wreck's sounds will be reenacted—although there are no cars to see, if you look down at the river you will see the ripples in the water as if an automobile just splashed in.

In my opinion—and it's just that—the legends around Screaming Bridge are just high school stories. The accident didn't happen on that bridge, and besides, both bridges associated with the story are now gone. When I asked Vicki about the ghost stories, she said, "I never heard the stories they are telling about the Screaming Bridge; that had to have happened after my school days. When I was in school it was shut down because it was too old. It had to be rebuilt, and now it is not even there anymore. You can't get to the site because the city closed down the road and built an alternate route to the Hurst-Euless-Bedford area. You can see the place where Screaming Bridge was from afar if you know where it used to be. The photo at the first of this chapter looks out into the location of the old bridge. Also, the bridge where the six kids went off trying to cross railroad tracks has been closed; you cannot get to it either. The new road that was built takes you away from that site."

The ghost stories of Screaming Bridge illustrate why it is important to examine the history of a haunted location. Occasionally, you will find that the actual facts on which the stories are based are flawed, which may be an indication that the associated haunting may be nothing more than a campfire legend.

I don't mind that the Screaming Bridge ghost stories probably aren't true—when looking for ghosts, it's just as important to identify the false stories as it is the true ones. My biggest regret is

The bridge often mistaken for Screaming Bridge

that the bridge isn't there anymore. I'd love to drive slowly across it one night, just to listen to the creaking and crackling that gave the bridge its name. Ghost or not, that would be one chilling experience.

Screaming Bridge
(removed several years ago)
Arlington, TX

# Bird's Fort—"Where the West Begins"

The way that people assign identities to ghosts never ceases to amaze me. If a spirit exists in our state capitol, it is immediately assumed to be that of Sam Houston or some other noteworthy statesman—never a janitor who might have spent his entire life there. Find a wandering phantom in the Alamo, and it has to be Davy Crockett, not some nameless patriot who gave his life during the horrific battle. So is the case with the spirit of Bird's Fort;

The site of Bird's Fort in the distance

when paranormal activity started occurring around this historic area, folks immediately assumed that it was Jonathan Bird himself.

Of course, when I started out, I had no idea who this Bird fellow was, only that I'd heard he was haunting some fort out in Arlington. That was enough to put it on my list to investigate for this book.

A trip to the Arlington Public Library uncovered the real story about the place, including the fact that Major Bird oversaw the building of the fort, but after that, left a garrison of men there and went ahead to bigger and better things. He built it and was gone, much like the construction companies of today.

There was so much trauma and bloodshed around the fort that whatever presence might walk the area today could be attributed to any number of people who, for whatever reason, just haven't moved on yet. It just probably isn't Jonathan Bird.

When I started digging a little deeper on the ghosts of Bird's Fort, I found out something very interesting: The fort site itself is not the source of the reported supernatural disturbances. That particular place is located on private property and is unavailable to the general public. The photo at the beginning of this story shows

the approximate view of where it was once located. The paranormal activity that actually has been reported is in the vicinity of the
site of the old fort, though, so it is collectively known as the "Bird's
Fort Haunting."

The background that I found on Bird's Fort itself was very
interesting, and maybe a little shocking. You see, I've driven
through the mid-cities of the Dallas/Fort Worth Metroplex many
times without a single thought as to what might have happened
before all the hamburger joints and car lots sprung up.

Back in the 1840s, there weren't any signs of civilization, not
even roads. Instead, there were established trails that had been
used by the Indians for years and had recently been adopted by
settlers and the military.

There were still problems with Indian raids at the time, a fact
which was hampering settlements in the area and greatly frustrating the military. Being part Cherokee myself, I don't really want to
get into the rights and wrongs of the actions of the Texas settlers—I've got relatives on both sides of the battle. By a very basic
definition, history is simply the facts of the way things happened
back then. It's important to look at these facts objectively when
investigating a haunted site.

But let's get back to Bird's Fort. As a precursor to the building
of the fort, a battle took place between three Indian tribes and the
Republic of Texas Militia on May 24, 1841. Just for the record, the
tribes were the Caddos, Cherokees, and Tonkawas. A famous man
was killed in the battle—one that will show up in a later chapter of
the book: John B. Denton, a Methodist minister and lawyer from
Arkansas. Denton's body was buried beside a creek bed, although
it was later moved to the city and county for which he was the
namesake. A dozen or so Indians were killed in the battle as well.

After the skirmish with the Indians, General Edward H.
Tarrant—the fellow that Tarrant County would later be named
after—ordered Major Jonathan Bird to take one hundred volunteers from the Fourth Brigade of Texas Militia and establish a
fortress. The fort was built in September and October of 1841 and
consisted of a wooden blockhouse with a stockade and trench

defenses. Several homes for settlers were constructed, both inside and outside of the stockade.

The word about the fort was put out to attract settlers, and one of the first to arrive was John Beeman, a farmer from Bowie County in far northeast Texas. He'd heard about the safety that the fort provided, and he thought that it would be a wonderful place to settle his family. Beeman inspected the fort then returned home to Bowie County to gather the rest of his kin. He brought back quite a few folks—not only his wife and ten kids (yes, I said TEN kids), but also his brother and two other families.

When the group arrived at Bird's Fort, they found that its supplies were almost completely gone, and the military personnel were almost out of food. Beeman and the settlers pooled the provisions they had left over from the trip and tried their best to make a go of the new homes.

Things were tough, and the Indian tribes just wouldn't yield the land. Although the Indians never actually attacked the fort, they harassed the settlers in frequent attempts to drive them away. One particular time, the surrounding grass was set on fire by the Indians to prevent wildlife from finding food around the fort, thereby forcing the men to take longer hunting trips away from the fort. You can guess where we're going from here.

One hunting trip was undertaken on Christmas Day of 1841 by a few of the settlers, including Wade Rattan and Solomon Silkwood. When they were about fifteen miles away from the fort, Indians ambushed the hunting party and killed Mr. Rattan. A party was dispatched to retrieve his body several days later, and they found it beside the creek where he had fallen. Rattan lay there dead, with his pet dog beside his body, faithfully standing guard. That dog will figure prominently in one of the ghost stories about the place that's coming up shortly.

Because of the exposure to the cold on that hunting trip, Solomon Silkwood took ill and later died. Silkwood and Rattan were buried not far from the fort. As legend has it, Rattan's loyal dog refused to leave the graveside where his master was laid to rest.

The plot of land grew to be an actual cemetery as more bodies were added—two men and a little girl from the fort were killed in an Indian ambush while fetching water from a nearby lake.

A last-ditch effort was made by the settlers when they tried to farm the land around the fort in 1842, but when their attempt failed, the survivors packed up their belongings and abandoned the place. Looking back, you have to wonder how they even lasted that long.

The fort sat empty for a year, but it made one final, glorious appearance in history on September 29, 1843. General G.W. Terrell and General E.H. Tarrant, commissioners on the part of the Republic of Texas, met with the leaders of ten Indian tribes. I'd never heard of some of them, but just to make the story complete, they were the Delaware, Chickasaw, Waco, Tawakoni, Keechi, Caddo, Anadarko, Ioni, Biloxi, and Cherokee. Their efforts toward peace brought about the Treaty of Bird's Fort, which ended all hostilities and established a border between Indian lands and the territory that was open for settling. This line of demarcation became known as "Where the West Begins," a slogan that soon became synonymous with the nearby city of Fort Worth.

The fort fell into ruins, and the ruins into the dust. Nothing more remains, at least nothing readily visible to the average passer-by. But reports of strange goings on began to surface from those living in the area or pausing to examine the lands surrounding the fort.

Several stories are told, but they all break down to one of three basic hauntings that seem to be taking place around Bird's Fort: a spectral man in simple frontier clothing, a phantom Indian warrior on horseback, and a lonely dog, howling for his lost master.

Let's start with the dog, because that is my favorite of the three. If you remember, one of the men who died in the fort area did so at the hands of a small band of Indians, who ambushed his hunting party. He'd brought a bulldog when he moved to the fort, and the dog was out hunting with them on that particular day. When the man was killed, the others fled, but they returned a few days later to retrieve the body. They found his bulldog beside the man, probably confused as to why his master wasn't waking up.

The settler was buried about two hundred yards away from the fort, with the bulldog watching the event solemnly. When the last shovel of dirt was packed onto the grave, the mourners slowly trickled away, but the dog stayed beside his fallen master.

I can't say whether the dog eventually wandered away, fell prey to predators there on the prairie, or grieved himself to death at the graveside. No matter what the outcome, I found several accounts of a lonesome, howling dog somewhere around the fort. As I mentioned, you can't visit the fort itself, but most of the traumatic experiences attached to the fort happened to people away from the structure. As visitors to the area walk the grounds that are accessible, a dog is sometimes heard howling in the distance. Those who know the legend have tried to find the animal, but he always seems just a little bit farther away. It could easily be that their common experience is a dog wandering its countryside home, or perhaps there is something more to the story. It might be that the grief of the loyal companion was so strong when his master was killed, the emotion lingers even to this day, in the form of a distant, forlorn howl.

The canine isn't the only spirit that is reported in the area, though. Another phantom is a man who, from his description, could easily be one of the settlers from Bird's Fort. This gentlemen is also most often reported from history buffs who are visiting the fort area to take photos, read the historical markers, and simply get a feel for all the history that surrounds Bird's Fort.

We've all had the feeling of being watched. That's the very thing some people report when they've left their cars and are hiking the areas along the fence line surrounding the fort that is available to the public. The occasional visitor is treated to more than an eerie feeling, though—a man dressed in simple, old-fashioned clothes stands a hundred yards away, acknowledging nothing, a silent sentinel from a bygone era. Turn away, and he'll be gone when you look back, but the feeling of his presence will remain. This gentleman, whoever he might be, is most often glimpsed out of the corner of a visitor's eye. A figure is detected in your peripheral vision, but when you look, there's nothing there but an empty field—but you know you're not alone.

The third and most rare of the three supernatural occurrences is the appearance of a mounted Indian warrior in full battle regalia. Stories of this phantom go back to the very days of the Old West itself, one of which is chronicled in Elaine Coleman's book *Haunted Texas Forts*. His mission seems to be one of helping women in trouble and reportedly frightened off attackers when a pioneer woman was falling prey to highwaymen and bandits. In our modern, civilized world, this spirit probably doesn't have the same opportunities he did 150 years ago, and reportings of this spirit are rare.

When I was visiting the Bird's Fort area, I have to admit I had a very odd feeling while wandering around the property that once held the "Site of Bird's Fort" historical marker. I didn't see the spectral pioneer man on that visit, but I felt like I wasn't alone. It could have just been the knowledge that so many things had happened there in the short history of Bird's Fort, but you never know. I decided to just to take a few minutes to soak in the historic old place and keep my ears open for the sound of a lonesome dog howling in the distance.

If you wanted to visit the Bird's Fort area, two Texas State Historical Markers were all that remained to remind us of Bird's Fort. Due to the construction along FM 157, however, both markers have been removed. These two markers gave concise histories of the fort and the people who once lived there. It may very well be, however, that a few of the original settlers, and perhaps some of their former-life adversaries, still remain, occasionally making their presence known to keep the memory of the fort and its history alive today. The text of the markers is as follows:

Historical Marker #1: "Site of Bird's Fort" (originally located 1 mile south of Calloway Cemetery Rd. on FM 157 in Arlington)

Marker Text: "Established in 1840 by Jonathan Bird on the Military Rd. from Red River to Austin. In its vicinity an important Indian treaty, marking the line between the Indians and the white settlements, was signed September 29, 1843, by Edward H. Tarrant and George W.

Terrell, representing the Republic of Texas. The ragged remnant of the ill-fated Snively expedition sought refuge here, August 6, 1843. (1936)"

Historical Marker #2: "Site of Bird's Fort (One Mile East)" (originally located on FM 157, 1 mile north of Trinity River, Arlington)

Marker Text: "In an effort to attract settlers to the region and to provide protection from Indian raids, Gen. Edward H. Tarrant of the Republic of Texas Militia authorized Jonathan Bird to establish a settlement and military post in the area. Bird's Fort, built near a crescent-shaped lake one mile east in 1841, was the first attempt at Anglo-American colonization in present Tarrant County. The settlers, from the Red River area, suffered from hunger and Indian problems and soon returned home or joined other settlements. In August 1843, troops of the Jacob Snively expedition disbanded at the abandoned fort, which consisted of a few log structures. Organized to capture Mexican gold wagons on the Santa Fe Trail in retaliation for raids of San Antonio, the outfit had been disarmed by United States forces. About the same time, negotiations began at the fort between Republic of Texas officials Gen. Tarrant and Gen. George W. Terrell and the leaders of nine Indian tribes. The meetings ended on September 29, 1843, with the signing of the Bird's Fort Treaty. Terms of the agreement called for an end to existing conflicts and the establishment of a line separating Indian lands from territory open for colonization. (1980)"

Bird's Fort is in Arlington in the area bounded by:
Trinity Blvd. on the north
Green Oaks Blvd. on the south
SH-360 on the east
FM-157 on the west

# The Treasure of Crystal Canyon

First things first: there is no credible evidence that a treasure is buried in Arlington, Texas. It is simply not true. Accept it. Embrace it. Do not grab your shovel and head for Arlington.

All that said, there is a very interesting story circulating among the ghost hunters in the mid-cities area of Dallas/Fort Worth, and it all supposedly started back in the middle 1800s. I'm going to tell you the tale the way I first heard it while researching this book, realizing that to all the historians reading this, it will be a lot like fingernails on a blackboard—but we'll get to that later.

There are several versions to the legend, but here is how the basic story goes: a famous—or perhaps infamous—soldier named Lt. Jacob Snively accepted an officer's commission for the Republic of Texas in 1836, just about the time a band of patriots were standing off against the Mexican army at a tiny mission down in San Antonio. The defeat of those men at the Alamo caused a swell of patriotism in the new republic, and Snively rode that wave to the rank of colonel by the time he was discharged eighteen months later. Texas had gained its independence, and Colonel Snively had made quite a name for himself.

Jacob Snively held many offices for the republic: paymaster general for the army, secretary of war under Sam Houston, and special plenipotentiary to the Indian tribes in the republic. In 1843 Snively petitioned the government of the republic for permission to lead a raiding party against Mexican wagons crossing through land that was claimed by Texas. Authorization was given, and so he mustered 100 to 150 men who gathered at Coffee's Station on the Red River. The band was so sure of their strength and success that they adopted the name "The Battalion of Invincibles" and unanimously elected Jacob Snively to be their commander. With a hearty roar, the men set off to find their prey.

One of their raids was so successful that it netted a shipment of Mexican gold, which the Invincibles brought back to Texas, heading toward Bird's Fort in what is now Arlington. The United States Army did not take kindly to their raid, however, viewing it

The sloping sides of Crystal Canyon

as an act of piracy against the Mexican government. The U.S. troops began to pursue the men into Texas, and rather than give up the gold, Snively and his men made a stand in a canyon several miles south of Bird's Fort. When it appeared that their cause was lost, Snively directed several of his men to bury the gold in the walls of the canyon, a task that was completed by the time that the United States soldiers overtook the Battalion of Invincibles' position. The dead were buried in the canyon, and the rest, including Jacob Snively, were turned over to officials of the Republic of Texas. Now would be a great time to strike up the mysterious music, as I further explain that the gold has never been found, although many prospectors and ambitious individuals have tried. Those who linger in the canyon after dark, however, have found more than they bargained for. Disembodied voices and footsteps make themselves heard and chase the intruders from the small canyon. These mysterious sounds are assumed to belong to the men who died there protecting the gold—a duty they seemingly perform to this very day!

Researching this haunting proved to be a very interesting task. First of all, the legendary canyon wasn't hard to trace. The ghost-hunters who first related the story to me pegged it as a place called "Crystal Canyon" in Arlington; there are also many Internet references to that location being haunted. With that in mind, it was off to do a little digging—of the paper kind—at the local library.

I discovered through many historical writings that Jacob Snively was definitely a historical figure in the Republic of Texas, and he actually did lead the Battalion of Invincibles. Although their charter was to intercept wagon trains from Mexico heading for the Santa Fe Trail, once the United States Army under Col. Philip St. George Cooke got wind of it, they challenged Snively's authority in the matter. Following a brief period of saber rattling, the Invincibles turned around to head back to the Texas settlement of Bird's Fort, and they disbanded in August of 1843. This is a prime example of how a few twists to a factual story can give birth to a whopping tale.

There is no way to determine how the legend of the ghosts and the gold got its start. Perhaps people in the area heard about Snively's plan to intercept Mexican wagons, learned of the interference by the U.S. troops, were told about the Invincibles being at Bird's Fort, and finally put that together with Snively's brief dealings with gold in New Mexico and Arizona, and so the gaps in the chain of events were filled in with elaborate fiction.

Whatever happened, people have believed the tale that gold was buried in the canyon for years. The land where "Crystal Canyon" is located was once owned by Holley Hale and was worked as a farm. One of her farm hands was reportedly kept busy chasing amateur prospectors away from the property.

The likelihood of this area being haunted is slim, if at all. As explained above, Jacob Snively never intercepted a gold shipment, and he never made a desperate stand against the U.S. Army in the area that is now Crystal Canyon.

A stronger case against it turned up in my research, however. I ran across an essay written by a man about growing up near Crystal Canyon. It was apparently a favorite place for neighborhood kids to gather and play, and the loving affection with which he recalled those days convinced me that he had spent many an hour there. If anyone knew of the legend of buried treasure, it would

The view through Crystal Canyon

certainly be a kid who spent that much time at the place. As far as I was concerned, that put the final nail in the treasure and ghost legend. I would have loved to include several passages from the essay, but it was apparently written several years ago, and although the author's name was attached, I was unsuccessful in locating him to obtain permission.

One thing I did do was to drive over to Crystal Canyon in Arlington, park my car at an apartment building across the street, and go exploring. The rock in the canyon is so soft that many people have carved into it. There were names, sayings, icons, and signs, all given some permanence by the fact that their message will last for years.

Don't get me wrong, however. I detest the defacing of property in any way, shape, form, or fashion. As I left the Crystal Canyon area, I couldn't help but chuckle, though. What if our civilization were to suddenly die out, only to be uncovered some eons later. These markers by teenage hands would be revered as some spiritual incantation, and a new religion would probably be built up around them. Stranger things have certainly happened.

The land is now owned by the city of Arlington and is being developed for a park. Ironically, for some time there have been signs posted in the Crystal Canyon area proclaiming: "Danger, Do Not Dig. Buried Fiber-Optic Cable Below." With the new technology that fiber optics brings us, maybe there is a treasure underneath the soil of Crystal Canyon after all!

Crystal Canyon Park
1000 Brown Blvd.
Arlington, TX 76011
(Park scheduled for completion in 2005)

# The Ghosts of Cleburne

**W**hen I visited Cleburne, I had two different places in my notebook to check out. Approaching the city, I saw a majestic courthouse standing up above the town, and I wondered why so many of the cities that I found to have hauntings were county seats. Maybe it is because those are some of the oldest towns in North Texas, I supposed, and Cleburne was no different.

As the center of county government, the city has its fair share of traffic and commerce today. Cleburne got its start on an old wagon trail, believe it or not. Soldiers traveling between Fort Graham and Fort Belknap passed through there, and because of the abundant water supply provided by Buffalo Creek, it became a frequent stop for civilian travelers from the Chisholm Trail as well.

Once the Civil War started, the city became the logical choice for the Confederate troops from Johnson County to bivouac before heading out to their assigned stations across the South, and the temporary facility soon attracted businesses that catered to the soldiers. The settlement became a permanent town in 1867, named after General Patrick Cleburne of the Confederate army, and was later appointed to be the county seat of Johnson County.

When the railroads came to Cleburne, so did industry, and the town has continued to have a steady growth.

I was in town long enough to do some research and even have a bite of lunch. Unfortunately, one of the haunted locations that I'd heard about was closed up and had a big "For Sale" sign out front. Unable to locate anyone associated with the property, I sadly abandoned my research on it and proceeded onward. The other location, the Wright Place, was located just a little ways from the courthouse and was easy enough to find. I decided to continue my exploration of Cleburne there.

# The Spectral Girl of the Wright Place

When is a haunted house *really* a haunted house? When it's the Wright Place in Cleburne, Texas. Okay, okay, let me explain. When I was swapping emails with former *Fort Worth Star-Telegram* writer Andy Grieser to ask about his experiences at Thistle Hill in Fort Worth, I discovered that he was part of another ghost investigation in Cleburne at a two-story structure known as the Wright Place. When Mr. Grieser's team showed up for their ghost hunt in 1996, they found the upper floor of the building was draped with Halloween decorations and signs proclaiming that it was the "Death Express."

As it turned out, the upstairs floor of the building was completely empty, and so for the spooky season it had been turned into a thrill house much like the kind of Halloween attractions that crop up all over North Texas in October. Not that I'm knocking them; for a few bucks, folks can get a good scare by a guy in a ghost sheet or vampire costume.

The staff for the "Death Express" had all gone home, though, and so Mr. Grieser's group had the place to themselves. They rolled out their sleeping bags and settled in for an evening on the upstairs floor, just to see if there was anything to the stories about the ghosts in the old building.

And old it is. It was originally built as a hotel, the Hamilton House, all the way back in 1874. There were twenty-five rooms, making it a fairly large place for the time. Cleburne needed the accommodations, though, because many travelers passed through on their journeys to the surrounding cities of Dallas, Fort Worth, and Waco. Since it was also the county seat, there was also a lot of legal and government activity there, attracting businessmen who needed a place to stay.

In 1916 a tragedy befell the hotel when a fire raged through the southern part of the building. Since the business of the hotel had started to fall off anyway, the owner decided to sell the building instead of going through all of the time and trouble to restore it. A gentleman by the name of Mr. A. J. Wright bought the building and

The Wright Place building

after a little work, had it put back together and ready for its new role as a mercantile store. People from all over the area drove their horse and buggies into town to restock with all the necessities and luxuries that a person could want: sugar and flour, canned goods, work clothes, and even penny candy for the youngsters. At that time the Wright Place was a thriving business and provided a much-needed service to the community.

Eventually, however, the store closed. Whether the market just became saturated with such businesses, or larger stores moved the mom and pop business out, the doors to Mr. A. J. Wright's store were locked a final time.

After that the building sat empty for several stretches, but through the years the downstairs housed any number of businesses. In 1996, when Mr. Grieser and his group paid their nocturnal visit to the place, the downstairs held "Pappy's Bar-B-Q and Soda Fountain." As I understand it, the barbecue sandwiches were outstanding! The entire way to Cleburne, I was looking forward to lunch there. I was weighing the merits of sliced beef versus chopped beef, or maybe going a bit healthier and choosing the turkey. Imagine my disappointment when I got there and saw that Pappy's was no more. There appeared to be other businesses on the first floor, so the building is at least still being used. Man, was my mouth set for barbecue, though.

With all the activities of commerce taking place on the first floor, there are many stories about activity of a different type occurring upstairs. Many unusual things have been reported over the years at the Wright Place on the second floor where people rarely ventured. When someone did go upstairs, an occasional touch on the shoulder would be a reminder that they might not be alone. It is never anything startling—just a brush, really, as if another person has passed by a little too close. In these cases, though, there was never anything, or anyone, even remotely close by.

Another indication that there could be a spectral presence up on the second floor is the sudden aroma of cigar smoke. People have described it as being a definite cloud of aroma that seemed to float around the top floor, as if a man was walking there with his stogie. No footsteps, no lumbering spirit figures of a gentleman from the past, just the smell of someone smoking a cigar that wafts though the air.

Yet another manifestation of the unseen things in the Wright Place was the laughter of children on the second floor. The sounds would emanate from the far corners when the building was empty. No one knew who the phantom kids were or why they were there, but their voices echoed out as if the group was frolicking through the building.

There is one spirit, however, that seems to be very intent on making herself known among all of the other supernatural things that happen on the second floor—the ghost a young girl who has been occasionally seen standing in an upstairs window. Although no one knows exactly who she is, many believe she is a red-haired young lady who worked in the hotel in 1882.

Most reports about the establishment paint it to have been a very reputable place. In a town that was host to every form of traveler from cattlemen to politicians, and trail hands to traveling salesmen, there may have been some shady transactions occurring at the hotel. There are reports that working girls frequented rooms at the old place to entertain such gentlemen, and if that was truly the case, then one of the girls may still be lurking around the second story of the Wright Place building.

Some say that a businessman tried to take advantage of one particular girl, a redheaded beauty who was merely a hotel worker, and as she struggled to get away from his clutches, she fell through an upstairs window and landed on the street below, broken and dead. Another story about the young lady puts a different light on things—one where she was a prostitute who worked out of a particular room in the Cleburn hotel, soliciting business from the men who came through town. After an encounter with a customer got a little out of hand one evening, a fight ensued between the girl and her client, and he ended up throwing her from a second-story window.

No matter who the girl was or how she died, the fact remains that her presence is seen and felt at the Wright Place. Not only is she seen in the window, but visitors to the upstairs sometimes pick up the scent of a citrus perfume in the air, heralding the fact that her spirit is in the old hotel once again.

As for Andy Grieser and his ghost expedition, well, they didn't see the redheaded lady of the hotel that night. What did happen, however, was a series of strange events that ranged from people in the group being touched by some unseen hand, to cold spots that were felt in different places on the second floor. When the wee morning hours wore on and things finally seemed to quiet down, the ghost hunters packed up their gear and headed for the house.

After the team left, the upstairs was opened again the next evening for the haunted house attraction, the "Death Express." It must have been a success because the following year, the haunted house reopened as "Faustus Sanatorium." And why not? A haunted house in a place that is really haunted would be the perfect mix—visitors might not be able to tell the difference between the costumed humans portraying ghosts, and ones that have crossed over but are simply back for a visit. You have to wonder if any of the "haunted house" patrons saw a red-haired girl dressed in 1800s garb standing near the window, looking out at the town, only to think that it was one of the actors trying to frighten them!

The Wright Place
#1 James St.
(one block south of the Johnson County Courthouse)
Cleburne, TX

# The Ghosts of Dallas

**W**ell, what can I say about Dallas—or "Big D," as people called it when I was a kid growing up in East Texas. I had two uncles and aunts along with three cousins all living there, so we came to visit often. I can still remember marveling at the huge shopping centers (they really didn't have the mega-malls at that time like we enjoy today). In fact, one of the grandest places I'd ever seen was Big Town, just off of I-30. And all of the lights at Christmas, well, don't even get me started. It was a wondrous place to a child.

My wife and I made the Dallas area our home almost twenty years ago, and even after all that time, I didn't know much about the origins of the city.

There's an old saying that "The painter's house always needs painting," and that's true with Dallas and myself. I was so busy looking at other places for travel and weekend getaways, that I'd never taken a close look at Dallas. With this book, I figured it was time that I did.

What I discovered about Dallas, the city I thought I knew so well, was that it was founded by a fellow named John Neely Bryan in 1841. He chose the location on the Trinity River because it was near a natural ford, making the settlement a perfect place to stop before or after crossing the river. Bryan wasn't the first person to discover the ford, however, because two major Indian trails went through there as well. There's more information about one in particular when we talk about the Preston Road ghosts.

By 1844 there were enough people moving to the town that a plan was laid out for streets and properties, and the founding fathers must have thought it was going to be a huge place, because they partitioned a whole square half-mile's worth.

Now, there seems to be a lot of question as to who the city of Dallas was actually named after. There are many names that you'll hear bantered around, including George Mifflin Dallas, who served in the office of vice president of the United States between 1845 and 1849. There are apparently several different stories, though, and the person telling each one has a hundred reasons why his is right. In all actuality, no one is sure how Dallas got its name.

The one thing everyone can agree on is that it was growing at an extremely fast pace. Dallas County was formed after the city of Dallas, so there again we have no factual evidence as to who the county was named after. It doesn't matter, though; Dallas (the city, not the county) was named as the county seat, winning over a neighboring town named Hord's Ridge. Hord's Ridge would later assume the more pleasant name of Oak Cliff and would eventually be swallowed up by the city of Dallas.

Simply stated, Dallas exploded at that point. People poured in, and it would be easier to list the businesses that Dallas didn't have than the ones it did. There were doctors, druggists, grocery stores, churches, dry goods stores, insurance agents, clothiers, you name it and Dallas probably had it. Since the Trinity River was basically unnavigable, railroads brought the commerce that was needed to carry the city to the next level.

A few of the haunted locations I found to explore in Dallas go much further into the history of the city, so I'll stop here and let the individual places tell the rest of the tale.

I had fun tracking them down, though, whether I was touring the impressive Sammons Center for the Arts or talking ghosts with the bartender at the Sons of Hermann Hall over a cold beer. While driving through downtown on my way to Old City Park, I happened to glance over at the skyline. I remember back when I was a little kid, maybe thirty-six years ago (wow, could it possibly have been that long?) when my folks and I would visit. The tallest building in the city was easy to spot, because it had a huge red Pegasus revolving at its peak. The flying red horse is still there today, but the building is dwarfed by the giants that have risen around it, and you have to know just where to look.

But I'm rambling—I could talk about Dallas all day. It would be much more fun, however, to continue on this ghostly journey, traveling from hamburger joints, to theaters, and even to the beautiful shores of White Rock Lake.

# The Spirits of Snuffer's Restaurant

When ghost hunting meets cheese-fries, you've got yourself one of the best hamburger joints in the Dallas/Fort Worth Metroplex, if not the entire state of Texas: Snuffer's Restaurant.

The original front entrance to Snuffer's

I've eaten there countless times over the years, always enjoying one of their delicious burgers or feasting with friends on a plate of their signature dish: cheese-fries piled high with bacon crumblings, scallions, and jalapenos. I defy you to eat an order by yourself!

For as long as I've lived in the North Texas area, Snuffer's has been a favorite place for friends to gather and visit—to have a few beers, have a bite to eat, and simply just enjoy an afternoon or evening out. After all those burgers I had enjoyed there, though, there was one thing that I'd never picked up on: When the lights were turned out and just a few people were left to close up the place, another presence or two made themselves known in the Greenville Avenue burger joint. You see, Snuffer's Restaurant is haunted.

The popular eatery was opened back on June 28, 1978, by Pat Snuffer, and the original restaurant only consisted of one room with fifteen tables and a service bar over in the corner. The menu contained the same basic entrees that it does today: burgers, sandwiches, and the house specialty of cheese-fries that helped make the diner famous.

The college crowd from Southern Methodist University discovered Snuffer's soon after it opened, and it quickly became a favorite stop on Greenville Avenue. As its popularity increased, the restaurant expanded to meet the needs by building another dining area behind the original restaurant. After this new addition opened, however, strange things started to happen at Snuffer's.

I'd heard this on a couple of occasions but never really thought anything about it, until I started gathering information for a book on haunted locations in North Texas—the very book that you're reading, as a matter of fact.

I found out about the ghosts from a waiter on one of my excursions there for lunch with a couple of friends. As he was setting our entrees on the table, I posed the question out of nowhere: "So, what can you tell me about the ghosts?"

The fellow looked at me as if I'd caught him completely off guard. "Wow, I've never had anyone ask me about that before. I thought only the people who worked here knew about it!"

We talked for some time, and he told me several interesting stories about the spirits that inhabit Snuffer's. There are apparently many things that happen there, but the most dramatic is an actual apparition that occasionally appears. "The ghost kind of drifts out of the hallway between the two dining rooms and comes a few yards into the new part, before it fades back into the hall. It's just a white form, really, not like a distinct person or anything. I've never seen it, but some of the folks here have."

As it turns out, both employees and customers have occasionally witnessed a hazy spirit walking the hallway between the old and new sections. Just as my friend the waiter described, an apparition would sometimes move out of the hallway and come a few feet into the new section then return to the hall, which seems to be the focus of some of the supernatural activity there. It's a narrow hall, sort of L-shaped with doorways to both the ladies' and gents' rooms along the way. In the original restaurant, this was at the back of the building, but now it is a connecting passageway between sections.

The hallway where one spirit is most active

Sometimes the entity that inhabits the hall isn't seen but is still very active. Footsteps have been heard in that hallway connecting the two sections of the restaurant when no one was there. On occasion, when things are very quiet, the door to the men's restroom is heard to slowly creak open, but oddly enough, it never closes back. My waiter explained it with one theory that has been passed around among the wait staff—in the days before Pat Snuffer bought the building, the place was a roughneck biker bar, and one of the patrons was stabbed in a fight that broke out in the back of the restaurant. He stumbled through the back and into the hallway then collapsed into the men's restroom, where he died right there in the doorway. His body was blocking the door, prohibiting it from closing.

Was there a fight in some old bar there on Greenville, and did the man really pass away in the hallway? There's no way to know for sure. After my conversation with the fellow at Snuffer's, I literally spent several hours in the library combing through the *Dallas Morning News* articles around that time period, but I could find nothing to substantiate the story. The fact remains, though, that a restless spirit seems to pace the small hall between the two sections of the building.

The hallway man isn't the only spirit at Snuffer's, however. The phantom spirit of a woman dressed entirely in black has also been seen drifting through the dining room, never stopping to acknowledge the earthly patrons there. Again, my new friend hadn't seen her, but he told me that many people had—including Pat Snuffer, the restaurant's owner. "She doesn't act like anyone else is around. She just walks through the room, ignoring everyone around her. I don't know if she even knows that the place is a restaurant or not."

These are the two spirits that manifest themselves as figures. Some of the activity at Snuffer's isn't as dramatic. Unless you knew the stories, you might even dismiss them without a second thought. Everyone who works there seems to have a story of something odd happening, though. The staff has walked into an empty dining room to find that the lights are gently swaying, as if they had been lightly tipped by the hand of some unseen passerby. Menus and table settings are put out in a standard fashion throughout the restaurant, yet occasionally they are moved around when no one is looking. Some of the wait staff have even reported mysterious, whispered voices that echo though the near-empty

The oldest dining room, another site of ghostly activity

building at night. Whoever the spirits might be, they are quite playful. I asked my waiter what he had experienced while working there, and he told me he'd had one of the most common experiences, where you are alone in one of the dining rooms and you'll feel someone brush past you, only to turn and see that no one is there.

My waiter excused himself with a smile, promising to come back to tell a few more stories when he got caught up with his other tables. That's something else about Snuffer's I have always loved—the staff working there aren't simply automatons that take orders and bring food. Each one has a unique personality to share, which makes a visit to Snuffer's unlike any other restaurant experience you're likely to have.

I was hoping to get to talk to Mr. Snuffer himself, but he wasn't in during that particular trip. I knew I'd be back again soon, though. Before my next visit I found an article in *The Dallas Morning News* on October 31, 1999, where Mr. Snuffer told the reporter that he didn't believe in ghosts before he opened the burger joint in June

1978, but by the following January, he knew the place was haunted. "I didn't want my kids to think Dad's nuts," he told the newspaper, "so I didn't talk about it 'til about 10 years ago." Mr. Snuffer explained that, "Manifestations have occurred on the south side of the restaurant, usually within a few days of mentioning incidents." He and his employees get cold chills, hear their names called three times, or feel a hand on their shoulders. After hours, glassware and ashtrays move or fall six or eight feet away from their original locations in empty rooms.

Is Snuffer's really haunted? Many people say it is, and like the waiter told me, everyone who works there has a story of one thing or another happening. Those people who simply visit, like me, are possibly hoping to see one of the phantoms for themselves. Although I haven't yet, I will continue my investigation. My addiction to their cheeseburgers demands it.

When you stop by, you may just have a supernatural experience at Snuffer's. Then again, maybe you won't, but I'd recommend a visit anyway. After all, it's worth the trip for a plate of cheese-fries just to find out.

Snuffer's Restaurant
3526 Greenville Avenue between Martel & Longview
Dallas, TX 75206
Phone: 214.826.6850
Web: http://www.snuffers.com

# The Lady of White Rock Lake

Ah, the good old days. I was sixteen years old and riding in the passenger side of my friend's red Camero with the windows down and the music from the eight-track player blaring. Life just doesn't get any better than that.

We'd been driving all over Texarkana, cruising the car lots looking for a particular automobile that my buddy had heard about. A friend of a friend of his had supposedly seen the car, a sleek,

White Rock Lake, with downtown Dallas on the horizon

black Corvette with a price tag of only a thousand bucks. As the story was told, the owner of the car ran it off the road one night and crashed down into a ravine. The poor soul died in the accident, and no one noticed the car for several weeks. Now, I'm trying not to get too graphic at this point, but let's just say that the decomposing body left an overly odorous presence in the Corvette.

The friend of a friend of my buddy had said that a local car dealer bought the vehicle at auction and made all the necessary repairs, but there was one lingering problem: they couldn't get the smell out. New seats were installed, the carpet was replaced, the interior was completely reworked. Still, the scent of death would not leave the car.

And so we drove from one car lot to another that night, searching for that thousand-dollar Vette. My buddy and I never found it, and we soon forgot about the legendary car. But not before we told a few people, of course—the tale was much too interesting, and besides, a friend of a friend of my buddy had seen the Corvette, so it had to be true.

What does all this have to do with the Lady of White Rock Lake? Well, I'm getting there. Stay with me just a minute or two longer. You see, the Corvette story was only a faded memory for many years, until I picked up a book in the early 1980s by a man named Jan Harold Brunvand. He had assembled a book of widely circulated tales that are told as the truth but in reality are just myths. On page 20 was the story of "The Death Car." Yep, my buddy and I had fallen prey to a phenomenon of the 20th century known as "urban legends," and it seems that the same story had spread from one coast to the other, with its roots in the fact that a friend of a friend had actually seen the automobile. Sometimes the type of car was different, or how the wreck occurred had changed a little, but the story was basically the same.

Now, on to White Rock Lake, and the famous spirit that walks its shores. It is a beautiful place. Stroll along its walkways on any given day and you will encounter joggers, bicyclists, children playing, and folks like me who are just there for a little peace and quiet from the hectic pace of city life.

The lake was constructed in eastern Dallas in 1910 as a water supply for the city. The planners were interested in its beauty as well as its functionality, so tree-filled parks were built along the shores of the lake, and a winding road traced its circumference along with many pedestrian and bike trails. It is truly a magnificent place, and one that I love to visit.

As the sun begins to set over the lake, you can go to one of the lighted ball fields in the area to catch a softball game, or head down to the Bath House Cultural Center for a live performance or some other artistic exhibition. If you're just out for a leisurely evening drive, though, be careful about picking up hitchhikers—you may encounter the lake's phantom spirit.

The legend of the Lady of White Rock Lake has been in more newspaper stories, Texas ghost books, local Halloween television specials, and on Internet websites than any of the Dallas Cowboy football players. Okay, maybe that's a stretch, but the old girl does get around. According to the legend, if you were to have an encounter with the ghost it would go something like this:

*You're driving around one of the lonelier parts of the lake on a particularly dark evening, when your headlights catch the figure of a young woman walking beside the road in a long, dripping wet party dress. Her hair is soaked, and she is carrying a pair of formal slippers*

One of the many trails around White Rock, where
the ghostly lady takes her legendary stroll

*as she trudges along in the grass on the shoulder of the road. She puts out her thumb as you approach, and since she definitely doesn't appear to be a threat, you stop and offer her a ride. The lovely young lady opens the rear door and climbs into the backseat, then she begins a tale of how her car was in an accident back down the road. The vehicle left the pavement and went into the lake, and she was thrown out into the water. The poor dear wasn't hurt, thankfully, but is concerned that her parents are worried about her being out so late. All she needs, the girl says with tear-glistening eyes, is a ride to her home. You nod sympathetically, and she gives you directions to one of the stately mansions looking out over the lake.*

*As you pull into the driveway that traverses the finely manicured lawn, you turn around to ask if you've found the correct house. Mysteriously, the girl has vanished! In the place where she was sitting, however, is a puddle of water on your seat cushion. You are understandably freaked out and decide to knock on the door of the house to at least talk to the people there. An old, white-haired man opens the door slowly, and after hearing your tale, shakes his head and gives you a sad smile. He explains that his daughter was killed when the car that she was in went into the lake several decades ago, but every year on the anniversary of her death, she appears to some motorist who is kind enough to offer her a ride home.*

That is how encounters with the Lady of White Rock Lake go. Unfortunately, it is impossible to find someone who actually picked up the girl. Or knocked on the door. Or had any encounter with a ghostly presence at the lake. When the story is told, however, it is always true—because it happened to a friend of a friend, just like my thousand-dollar Corvette story.

The title of the book by Brunvand that I mentioned earlier is, *The Vanishing Hitchhiker: American Urban Legends and Their Meanings.* As it turns out, most every city with a lake nearby has a similar story of a young hitchhiking girl who vanishes in the car. Another variation features the poor thing knocking on the door of a home by the lake, asking to use the phone, then disappearing and leaving a puddle on the front porch. Yet another has her approaching young couples whose cars are parked out by the lake. Unfortunately the Lady of White Rock Lake, just like the Death Car that my buddy and I were looking for, is an urban legend.

Still, I didn't want to slight my readers, so I decided that the only prudent thing to do would be to give the ghostly gal a chance. I headed out for White Rock Lake, timing it so that the sun would just be setting when I arrived. As always, there were several people there, even though the crowd was thinning out because it was getting dark. I started out on the east side of the lake at Casa Linda shopping center then went southwest on Garland Road and turned right to get to the lake. There are several roads into the park area at the south end of White Rock Lake, and I cruised them all, just in case the water-soaked girl was hanging around down there. No such luck.

I wasn't about to give up, though, so I hopped back on Garland Road for a bit then left it again to follow Lawther Road up the western side of the lake. If there really is a ghost, she certainly wasn't looking for a ride on that particular night. I was pretty much alone.

The shores of White Rock Lake

On the north side I picked up Northwest Highway and made a stop on Flagpole Hill. While researching the Lady of White Rock Lake story, I came upon a few additional notes about the area. The first was that Flagpole Hill was supposed to be a place where Satan worshippers hung out, and that rocks would fly though the air at you, thrown by some invisible force. After exploring the area on foot, I gathered the following statistics:

Satan Worshippers: 0
Invisibly Hurled Stones: 0
Drenched Young Female Hitchhikers: 0

Another item I'd heard about was that there is a bridge on Lawther where, if you stop as you cross over, your engine will die. I stopped on every bridge I encountered, Lawther Road and otherwise, and my engine never died. On the other hand, maybe the guys at my local garage who keep my car in shape wield more power than the spirits on the bridge. One never knows.

Realizing that my trek would soon be over, I continued down Lawther along the east side of the lake, keeping my eyes peeled for anyone thumbing a lift. Alas, there was not a soul there, except for an occasional evening jogger with his reflective sneakers and headband.

I finally got on Buckner and headed back down to Casa Linda, a little disappointed. Not in the fact that I hadn't picked up the ghost—I never had any real expectations of finding the Lady of White Rock Lake. It just reminded me of that night back in Texarkana, driving home with my buddy, speculating how we'd get the smell out if we ever found the thousand-dollar Vette.

White Rock Lake
Dallas, TX

# The Wandering Spirits of Preston Road

Preston Road traverses Dallas from north to south and is traveled by literally thousands of people going about their business, oblivious to its history and the spirits that remain there. But could any ghost be brave enough to travel this dangerous byway? After all, on a daily basis, it frightens many of the living!

Preston Road, stretching from downtown Dallas northward to the outer suburbs, is arguably one of the busiest thoroughfares in the Dallas/Fort Worth Metroplex. In fact, publications such as *CNN, Road & Track Magazine,* and *USA Today* have all counted several portions of Preston Road as some of the most dangerous intersections in the country. State Farm Insurance even weighed in on the subject, naming Preston Road one of the nation's most treacherous thoroughfares. Standing beside the roadway today, it is incredibly hard to imagine how it must have appeared hundreds of years ago.

If you're like me, you probably assume that the road was constructed several decades ago when the city of Dallas began to grow northward. The thoroughfare that we call Preston Road

Preston Road at an uncharacteristically calm moment

today is older than the city of Dallas, though. Not only that, but it is also older than the state of Texas, the Republic of Texas, and even the United States of America. With something that old, it's no wonder that there are ghost stories associated with it!

Preston Road was originally a pre-Columbian Indian trail, traveled by the ancient people in their journeys to traverse the continent. Later on the Shawnee tribe adopted it as a path from what is now south Texas to the upper regions of the land. In 1838 the Republic of Texas authorized finances to survey a road from Austin, the capital, to the Red River territory. The Shawnee trail was a natural selection, and Colonel W. G. Cooke began the survey in 1840. In October of that year, he crossed the Trinity River, not far from the present-day location of downtown Dallas, and continued north.

The trail that Cooke was surveying led to a military post located near the Red River. The fort was named for Captain William C. Preston, an officer and veteran from the Texas Revolution. Cooke's trail soon became known as "Preston Trail," then "Preston Road," and eventually grew into the frantic thoroughfare that it is today.

Still, there may be some remnants of the past holding onto the history of the trail. Ghostly figures have reportedly been seen walking along Preston, especially between Spring Valley and Belt Line Roads. These specters are dressed in clothes of a century past and are making their way north, as if on a twilight trek to Fort Preston.

I can't imagine how anyone would notice them with all of the traffic whizzing by, but I decided to give the spirits a chance. All in all, I made three trips to Preston Road to look for ghosts: one on a Saturday afternoon, when the traffic was moderate; another on an early Tuesday morning just in time for rush hour; the final one I made just before midnight to find a time when the traffic had thinned out considerably. On each of the occasions, I walked the shoulder between Spring Valley and Belt Line, hoping to see some of the pioneer spirits. It was a nice little hike—who says ghost hunting isn't good exercise!

The rush hour visit was just plain crazy. I spent more time worrying that I was going to be nailed by some passing automobile than looking for ghosts, and if you've ever traveled that road in the early morning, you know what I mean. I don't think I've ever seen so many people in such a hurry! I feel compelled at this point to recommend against trying this yourself. It's not for the faint of heart.

The most interesting visit was the late evening trek. There were fewer cars, and I was able to actually stop and reflect on the history of Preston Road. If nothing else, it was very interesting to imagine that I was walking in the very footsteps of ancient bands of Indians as they headed northward. While I was doing this, something interesting happened. I was crossing over a bridge and caught a glimpse of something on the other side of the road. I'd like to say it was grayish and moving in the opposite direction, but it was just a peripheral sight out of the corner of my eye. When I turned my head there was nothing there. Most likely, it was the moonlight reflecting on the bridge's metal railing, or the glimmer of an approaching car's headlights.

The most entertaining visit was on a Saturday afternoon. After making a non-eventful trek along the roadside, I stopped into a burger joint to get a soft drink. Two Dallas police officers were seated inside, having a late lunch, so I decided to get the opinion of someone who drove Preston Road for a living. After procuring a diet cola, I approached the officers and introduced myself. There's just no elegant way to broach the subject, so I dove right in: "I'm doing research for a book about haunted places in North Texas, and I've been told that Preston Road has a few ghosts that walk along it dressed in pioneer clothing. Have you guys ever heard of anything like that?"

They looked at me, glanced at each other, and then both kind of smiled before one of them replied, "You mean *real* ghosts? Out on Preston Road?"

"Yep, right out there. I've walked the roadsides between Spring Valley and Belt Line, but I haven't had any supernatural experience at all. I just wondered if you guys have ever seen anything like a ghost beside the road, or had any reports like that."

The officer laughed and said, "If you're not careful out there, you may be the next ghost, with the way some of those people drive!"

We had a nice visit, and even though they were interested in the ghost story and asked a lot of questions about the book, neither had heard or seen anything that could be of help with the Preston Road ghosts.

It was a little frustrating, and I was starting to wonder how the ghosts of Preston Road stacked up against known fraudulent ghost stories such as the Lady of White Rock Lake, or the Screaming Bridge, both of which are covered in other chapters in this book. The one thing that kept me interested in this tale was that I did find multiple sources of information about it, and none of them contradicted each other, as did the different versions of the White Rock Lady. There were also no telltale signs of high-school legends, such as honking your horn at a certain time or place like in the Screaming Bridge stories. Of course, that still doesn't lend any extra credibility to the Preston Road ghosts, but it doesn't send up any red flags either.

I went home and got on an Internet ghost chat just to see if I could locate anyone who'd seen the spirits. Although many people had heard of the ghosts, no one online at the time had actually experienced them. One fellow was even proclaiming that he was going to drive over to Preston Road to see if he could find them. But unfortunately, spirits work on their own schedules, not ours. It was no surprise to me when he posted a follow-up note saying there were no ghosts there when he drove by.

I was just about to shut the computer down when one fellow told me he'd heard that the ghosts were "corner people"—ghosts that you'd catch in the corner of your eye. It made me rethink what I'd seen that evening on the bridge. Maybe it hadn't been a reflection after all, or perhaps it was just wishful thinking on my part.

In any case, no one seems to know who these spirits are. From all reports, they seem oblivious to the traffic rushing by, and they'd have to be to choose Preston Road as a place for an earthly appearance. If you are driving down Preston, however, and happen to catch the glimpse of these wandering figures as the sun starts to set on North Dallas, there is no need to stop. They'll be gone before you can even turn your head completely, even as they continue on some perpetual northern journey.

Preston Road
Between Spring Valley Road and Belt Line Road
Dallas, TX

# The Dark Man of the Lizard Lounge

Ask anyone in the theatrical world, and they'll tell you that every theater has a ghost—and the Grand Crystal Palace was no different. There is a twist to this tale, however. When the final curtain came down on the theater years ago, the spirits that stalked the dressing rooms and aisles apparently decided to stay.

This is a classic haunting, and it fascinated me to no end. As the location changed hands several times over, the ghosts continued to make themselves known, and each new business had to

The Lizard Lounge

reconcile itself to the fact that it had inherited a spirit with the property.

The building was initially constructed as a warehouse at the turn of the twentieth century in the area that is now the Deep Ellum section of Dallas. Who owned the warehouse and what kind of business was transacted there is not known, only that it was a place of commerce and storage. As things sometimes go, the place fell on hard times and the owners were forced to board the structure up. The area had many empty buildings, and the West End section of Dallas was starting to dry up as well, so there was little hope for rejuvenating the old warehouse or selling the building. It sat there neglected for many years.

Several decades later, however, a theater company discovered the building and quickly set out to transform it into an elegant showplace for the arts. Off-Off-Broadway playwright Molly Louise Shepard was one of the actresses who graced the stage there, so I set out to find her to ask a few questions. She's far away from Dallas now, but with the magic of email, we corresponded, and she was kind enough to share her information with me.

Ms. Shepard remembers her days at the theater back around 1985, and how beautiful the place was. Two of the most impressive items of the time were a one-hundred-year-old Steinway grand piano and a Baccarat chandelier hanging above it on center stage. The word around the theater was that the chandelier reportedly cost seven thousand dollars.

"Behind the piano was a huge, beautiful art nouveau stained glass panel depicting a maiden walking in a garden, entitled *Spring*." Ms. Shepard added, "that was also many years old. There were two grand stairways that sloped towards the stage from the balcony seating area, and many antiques and old paintings in the theatre. One was of a pretty young girl in Victorian clothes. She looked very much like Alice from the Lewis Carroll stories. That painting was reportedly haunted, but with a *good* spirit."

The tales of the Grand Crystal Palace ghosts circulated among the actors. Ms. Shepard recalled the rumor that several workers had been killed there when the space had been a warehouse, and that those spirits haunted the building. There was also a tale of a figure of a man in a turn-of-the-century black suit, with a black cape and hat, who haunted the audience area. According to her, "This spirit had a frightening or *dark* aura. It was very hard to be in the audience area of the theatre all by oneself, as I remember. I remarked on that 'creepy' feeling in that part of the building one day to a fellow actor, while waiting for rehearsal to begin. He explained to me the rumors of the different *haints* that populated the Grand Crystal Palace."

Like most haunted places, if you are there frequently enough, you will began to notice traces of the supernatural events that happen there. It wasn't long until Ms. Shepard began to have her own experiences at the theater, although hers wasn't a subtle occurrence! "One day," Ms. Shepard said, "I got to the theater before all of the other actors, and I went up to the dressing room alone. When I entered the room, the dressing table lights, well, for lack of a better word, simply *exploded*! I was pitched into total blackness. Panicking, I ran down those rickety old stairs in the dark, all the way down to the kitchen at a breakneck pace!" There was no explanation as to why this happened, and in fact, had it been strictly an isolated event, one might dismiss the whole thing as faulty wiring or the like.

Several other incidents convinced her that perhaps the stories about the spirits were real. "The next time I was in the dressing room alone, I was sitting at a dressing table mirror. Suddenly, an unplugged blow dryer picked up—all by itself—and flung itself clear across the room, right at my head!" There were other interesting things that happened, but possibly none so profound as the last one. The theater was experiencing financial troubles, and all signs pointed to an untimely end. The spirits might have known that. Ms. Shepard remembers, "The last time I was in the dressing room alone, I was waiting for the show to begin, and an overwhelming feeling of sadness came over me. I began to weep. After I gained composure and repaired my makeup, I went downstairs in time to make my entrance. I had a solo, 'My Ship.' I loved that song." And, unfortunately, the theater did close, but only after a host of actors and playwrights brought many wonderful nights' entertainment to Dallas.

Another entertainment spot named The Empire Club took over the building, and it subsequently closed. The next business to occupy the building tried to bring its own brand of amusement to the city. It was a "gentleman's club" named the *Gold Club Topless Cabaret*. With all my digging for information, I couldn't find out anything about those years, only that the place existed. I guess the patrons and employees there would like to remain anonymous. I can only imagine that the spirits must have been witness to a completely different atmosphere in the dressing room!

The adult establishment eventually shut down as well, and the current incarnation of the building came into being: a megapopular nightclub named the Lizard Lounge. A favorite of the late night crowd, the dancing and partying often continues until four in the morning—sometimes with the ghosts of the old Grand Crystal Palace. A regular at the Lizard Lounge, Mnemonyss has often experienced the spirits there. "As far as the *dark man*, as some call him, I saw him once as I simply scanned the stage area on the stairs that approach the dressing room. Something caught my perception, and when I glanced again, he was gone. This was all within the blink of an eye. I could see no features, merely something like a dark shadow with masculine appearance by its silhouette."

Others have seen the shadowy man. "A friend of mine has seen the apparition a few times as well. I feel that more spirits are about the place than the one that tends to show himself," Mnemonyss says. "I feel he likes the atmosphere, and likes to watch or enjoy it somehow. I definitely do not get any negative vibes from him."

So who are the spirits that haunt this warehouse, theater, strip joint, and finally, nightclub? Could they be the ghosts of the workmen who died in the building during its early days? Perhaps, although Mnemonyss gets a different feeling: "I really have no idea of the history of the building but have gotten images of organized crime from around the 1940s or '50s." No matter who these ghosts may be, they have been with the structure for many years, and they seem to be intent on staying, because things continue to happen there. As Mnemonyss says, "There have been times I have felt someone whisper in my ear and turn to find myself alone, no one anywhere near me."

The Lizard Lounge
2424 Swiss (at Good Latimer)
Dallas, TX
Phone: 214.826.4768
Web: http://www.thelizardlounge.com/

# The Phantom Ballroom of the Hotel Adolphus

Elegance. Style. Luxury. These are only a few of the words that describe the Hotel Adolphus in downtown Dallas.

When I first walked into the lobby, I quickly forgot I was there looking for ghosts. The scent of fresh flowers seemed to drift from every corner, and the music from a beautiful 1893 Steinway piano

The regal entrance to the Hotel Adolphus

took me back to a time long ago. It is played every day at afternoon tea. I couldn't help but be impressed by the rich paneling, Brussels tapestries, and English Regency furniture. Portraits of royalty adorn the walls: Her Royal Highness, Queen Elizabeth II of Great Britain with Prince Philip, and just around the corner, the king of brewers, Adolphus Busch.

The idea for the hotel first came to life back in 1910, when the city fathers of Dallas decided their city-on-the-grow needed a first-class, elegant hotel to serve the needs of its visitors. The name of Adolphus Busch was brought to their attention, since he had just completed the Oriental Hotel in Dallas. It had a reputation for being one of the finest hotels in the country at the time, a fact that led the delegation to St. Louis to meet with Mr. Busch.

Now, you may have recognized the name at this point, because it graces not only a very popular pilsner beer, but also one of the NASCAR stock car racing series.

When the folks from Dallas stood in Mr. Busch's office, he listened intently to their request, and after careful consideration and

negotiation, agreed to their proposal. There were only two stipula-
tions: several businessmen from the city would agree to invest in
the project, and he would be allowed to build it anywhere in Dallas
that he wished. Both requests were gladly met, and Busch traveled to Dallas to find the site.

Adolphus Busch was already very familiar with the great state.
Its citizens certainly enjoyed his beer, and in fact, Texas was the
first state to which Busch's brewing company shipped their frosty
beverages in refrigerated rail cars, just to get the product there
fresh. He owned several properties in the state and even in the
city of Dallas, so it didn't take him long to decide on a location for
the new hotel.

There's an old saying in town that "Adolphus Busch didn't
fight city hall, he bought it!" The site he selected for the new hotel
was Dallas' four-story city hall, which had been built in 1889. True
to their word, the city fathers had the building demolished and
cleared to give Adolphus room to work his magic.

The St. Louis architectural firm of Barnett, Haynes and
Barnett were enlisted to design the hotel, and Busch's son-in-law
Edward Faust took a break from his vice presidential duties at
Anheuser-Busch to oversee the entire operation.

On October 5, 1912, the regal Hotel Adolphus opened its
doors. When everything was said and done, the "Beer Baron
Baroque" building had cost Busch $1.87 million, but everyone
agreed it was worth it. The American Institute of Architects
declared it "the most beautiful building west of Venice." At
twenty-one stories, it was the tallest building in the state of Texas
at the time and remained so for many years. Legend has it, by the
way, that the number of floors came from the fact that Adolphus
Busch was the twenty-first of twenty-two brothers all involved in
the art of beer and winemaking. His profession left a mark on the
hotel as well, with a turret that was built to emulate a beer stein
and a chandelier emblazoned with hops and the eagle from the
Anheuser-Busch logo.

Mr. Busch never had the opportunity to stay at his namesake
hotel, however. He died on October 10, 1913, at Villa Lily, his cas-
tle on the Rhine that he had named for his wife.

The beer stein spire on the top of the Adolphus

The Busch family continued to hold the hotel until 1949, when they sold it to real estate magnate Leo Corrigan. The hotel passed into the hands of Noble House Hotels and Resorts in 1980, and in 1981 underwent an $80 million restoration. That same year it was named to the National Register of Historic Places, and in the following years it gathered virtually every architectural, interior design, and hospitality award in the industry. AAA gave the hotel a four-diamond rating, and its French Room restaurant is one of very few five-diamond restaurants in the nation. Adolphus would have been mighty proud.

The hotel's guest list reads like a who's who in America: royalty, presidents, entertainers, sports figures, and even astronauts. Franklin and Eleanor Roosevelt were guests of the Adolphus while attending the 1936 Texas Centennial Exposition. Silent film star Rudolph Valentino stayed there, as did band leader Tommy Dorsey, and even Queen Elizabeth II and Prince Philip of Great Britain. Nicholas Cage, John Woo, Bill Cosby, and Mary Higgins Clark are only a few of the present-day celebrities who have checked into the hotel for a pampered stay.

The "Living Room Lobby"

There are a few hotel guests, however, that seem to be staying there permanently. The stories have circulated for years, among both the staff and the guests of the hotel.

Mr. Davis told me, "I've never seen or heard anything myself, but apparently we may have a phantom ballroom. Many years ago there really was a nineteenth-floor ballroom that has since been converted into two suites. Over the years, as the story goes, we've occasionally had someone in those suites call down to the desk and ask us to kindly tell the people in the next room to turn down the music. Then we've found out the room next door is unoccupied—and, of course, there is no room upstairs."

It has happened enough, according to Mr. Davis, that a poem about the haunting is well known among hotel employees:

### The Phantom Ballroom

*At the Adolphus there's a ballroom*
*On the 19th floor, upstairs.*
*Its phantoms trace the dances*
*Of Ginger Rogers and Fred Astaire.*

*Guests sometimes hear the music*
*As the ghostly band plays on.*
*But the sophisticated goblins*
*Know to heed a soft baton.*

*Their object is to entertain;*
*No guest would they disturb.*
*They simply seek some warm applause,*
*With maybe one "Superb!"*

*Though now the ballroom's hidden*
*(It's become a pair of suites),*
*The spirits mind the music*
*And move deftly to its beats.*

*So, tonight at the grand Adolphus,*
*You are invited to tap your toe,*
*When the 19th floor is jumpin'*
*With the "swing" of long ago.*

What orchestra is playing those mysterious, melodic strains in the evening, and are there ghostly couples dancing the night away in the area that used to be the old ballroom? No one knows for sure. In an elegant place so richly steeped in history, though, it is easy to imagine a spirit or two deciding to settle in for a while.

As I walked across the lobby to leave, I had to stop and look over my shoulder when I heard the piano start up again, just to see who might be playing.

The Adolphus Hotel
1321 Commerce St.
Dallas, TX 75202
Phone: 214.742.8200
Toll Free: 800.221.9083
Web: http://www.hoteladolphus.com

# The Pioneer Ghosts of Old City Park

Just south of downtown Dallas, across I-30, is a thirteen-acre wooded park that is a time machine for its visitors in the guise of a small turn-of-the-twentieth-century town. As you explore it, you will find homes of various architectural styles: a simple dog run, a one-room-wide shotgun house, a Greek Revival mansion, and Queen Anne style homes. There are businesses in this tiny town, as well: a print shop with a cast-iron front, a classic small-town bank, the General Store, a blacksmith shop, and more. Public buildings include a Methodist church, a Greek Revival school-house, a train depot, and a typical hotel catering to drummers, or traveling salesmen of the time.

The interesting thing is that every one of these buildings is an authentic structure, lovingly and meticulously moved from every corner of North Texas to the park. The buildings were then enhanced with a total of over 25,000 historic artifacts dating from 1840 to 1910. To round out the experience, the town is staffed with craft persons and historians who demonstrate cooking, black-smithing, weaving and more. They provide information about the time period, the architecture, and many other fascinating points about the pioneer way of life.

The Dallas County Heritage Society offers tours to the public and to school classes, along with special seasonal events such as the Old Fashioned Fourth of July and the Christmastime Candle-light at Old City Park. If you're hungry during your visit, you'll enjoy sitting down for a delicious lunch at Brent Place Restaurant, located in an 1876 farmhouse. It wasn't mealtime when I was there, but one thing I noted was that they served a New York Cheesecake with Melba sauce, and in my opinion, that's appropri-ate any time of day. No matter what I found with the ghosts, I knew there was going to be a slice of cheesecake in my future.

Old City Park is also Dallas's oldest park. It is on land originally purchased in the late 1840s by Lucy Jane Browder. Between the years of 1876 and 1885, the city of Dallas acquired about nineteen acres of the land and established the first city park, and they

named it just that: "City Park." Over time the luscious green grounds were landscaped with flowers and walkways, a small zoo was constructed, and a swimming pool and tennis courts were added for public enjoyment.

What happened next is pure Dallas legend, and I love it! As the story goes, an antebellum home was scheduled for demolition on February 18, 1966, in the name of progress. A group of strong-minded women put on their Sunday best clothes and makeup that morning and looked as beautiful as the day is long. In a rather un-dainty fashion, though, the group stood out on the front porch of the marked house that fateful morning, defying the construction crew to dare and bring their bulldozers onto the property. I imagine they were more than a little intimidating, and Lord knows I would have switched the machinery right off and left the premises. The foreman would have had to mow the house down himself, if he had the nerve to do so.

The ladies won the day, of course, and they quickly formed the organization now known as the Dallas County Heritage Society to try to prevent other such buildings from being demolished. That original home was relocated to City Park, signaling the start of a new community role for the place. Some land was lost when I-30 was built, and the swimming pool and tennis courts were eventually moved out. In 1971 the Heritage Society began seeking other historical structures to add to the park, and they began to lay out the area to become the turn-of-the-twentieth-century town and living museum that it is today. The name was changed to Old City Park in 1976, as part of was Dallas's first United States Bicentennial project.

Millermore Mansion

But the story of the park doesn't end there. With the houses that were moved in came some residents whose presence wasn't readily apparent. Strange occurrences were soon observed in two of the buildings: the Millermore Mansion and the Law Office. *Life Adventures*, the Internet travel and recreation magazine (www.lifeadventures.com) caught up with Hal Simon, the curator of Old City Park, to ask a few questions about the ghosts. In their March 2001 issue, Simon describes the activity at the Millermore, a Greek Revival style house built between 1855 and 1862 by William Brown Miller. "People say the back hall and the nursery area make them feel nauseated," Simon told LifeAdventures.com.

"They say there's a woman pacing back and forth. Visitors, our security and maintenance staff, and our volunteers have, at different times, all been a little spooked by the upstairs of the house. There have been enough stories that it makes you wonder."

The tales apparently have some effect on the staff at the park. Catherine Cuellar, in her Halloween day article "Favorite Haunts" in *The Dallas Morning News*, reported that when Mr. Simon is unlocking Millermore, "He might yell upstairs to announce his arrival, even though he knows the building is empty."

So who is this woman who seems to still live in the mansion? Many think it is the spirit of Minerva Barnes Miller, the wife of William Brown Miller. He began construction in 1855 as a home for him and Minerva, but she died a year later, before the house was complete. Could it be that because Minerva never got to live in the completed house during her life, she occasionally visits there in death?

No one knows for sure, but many people have reported a presence in the nursery they can't explain, including Old City Park office administrator Deborah Lister. As for being able to feel the presence herself, Ms. Lister told *The Dallas Morning News*, "No matter if we can explain it away, it's funky. All the women in my family are like this. I've grown up with it. It's also something that you just don't talk about."

But several have reported a figure in the upstairs window, to which Ms. Lister concurs. "Looking at the glass, you see someone standing with her hands together, in a dress, and the dress is light-colored. You can follow it up and make out details of the dress, and if your eyes come up, you run into where the face is. Almost everyone I can point it out to can see the hands in front of the dress in the bottom center pane. It's pretty recent that this manifestation has happened."

The ghostly lady in the Millermore is not the only spirit at Old City Park, however. The building called the "Law Office" was actually a neighborhood grocery store located at the corner of Oak and Nussbaumer Streets in East Dallas. In 1929 a mob murder reportedly occurred in the grocery, which may be the source of some of the activity there. The building has now been outfitted to represent a law office in a pioneer town. Mr. Simon described it to LifeAdventures.com: "The biggest problem we have with the Law Office is the security system in the building. The security boxes and panels have been replaced a number of times over the last six years while I've been here. The systems are replaced and within a week or so they will register that they've been tampered with."

The "Law Office"

I walked around every building in the park, drifting through some, studying the outside architecture of others. While I didn't have any ghostly experiences, I could feel the history in each and every one. At the Millermore, however, I took the time to sit out front in the shade of one of the trees and contemplate the haunting. I stared up at the upper windows, hoping to see a shadowy figure there, but I never did.

As I said at the first of this chapter, a spirit there at Old City Park makes me question the nature of ghosts. I've heard of buildings that are haunted because of the site on which they were built, but in this case, when the house-movers relocated the structures to the park, the ghosts came along for the ride! So, do ghosts haunt specific geographic locations, or the buildings that sit upon them?

Maybe the answer is "both," depending on the individual spirit. Just as they manifest themselves in different ways, perhaps they are each attached to something specific from their earthly life, be it a house, a location, or whatever else.

Pretty heavy thinking for a Saturday afternoon—something I decided would be much better done over a slice of New York Cheesecake with Melba sauce at the Brent Place Restaurant there in Old City Park. Since it was only a few buildings over from the Millermore, I picked up my notebook and camera and walked away. I couldn't help but glance back over my shoulder a few times, though, just to see if any hazy form was peeking out of an upstairs window in my direction.

Old City Park
1717 Gano Street
Dallas, TX 75215
Phone: 214.421.5141
Web: http://www.oldcitypark.org

# Lonesome Spirit of the Sammons Center

One of the ways I researched this book was to sift through the archives of North Texas newspapers. I spent countless hours of library time, and every so often, I'd have a breakthrough and get a lead. On even rarer occasions, that lead would turn into something absolutely wonderful—such is the case with the Sammons Center for the Arts.

When I first contacted Joanna San Angelo, director of the Sammons Center, she told me, "We do indeed have some strange occurrences here from time to time. They are mostly centered around the elevator, although the actual sightings of our ghost have always been in other parts of the building. There's nothing scary or creepy about him, though; he appears to be lonely and craves company!" It sounded wonderful, and I knew I would be in

The Sammons Center

for a treat. We scheduled an appointment, and I set out to do my homework on the Sammons Center.

The building itself was designed by the Dallas architectural firm of C.A. Gill & Sons in an Italian/Romanesque style, and it was opened in 1909 as the Turtle Creek Pump Station. You'd now consider it to be a part of downtown Dallas, but back then it was way out on the edge of town by the Trinity River. The station was the sole source of water for the city of Dallas until 1930.

In 1930 the pump station was retired by the Dallas Water Utilities Department, having become obsolete, although it was maintained for some of the other department functions. Over time the Trinity River was rerouted to make way for Stemmons Freeway, and the building was eventually abandoned. For the next twenty to thirty years, it stood empty beside the freeway, being slowly overtaken by vines and vegetation and slipping away into ruin.

In 1981 the Sammons Center for the Arts Coalition was formed for the purpose of restoring the pump station back into a functioning entity. It was designated as a historic landmark by the Dallas City Council, and the group led by Joe M. Dealey Sr. and

John M. Stemmons began to see some promise for the old building. It reopened in 1986, this time as a home to nonprofit arts organizations. Strange, unexplainable things began to happen almost immediately.

"The building had a basement," Ms. San Angelo told me, "but we had to fill it in during the restoration. Water seepage made it unusable. In fact, the only part of the basement that wasn't filled is the elevator pit."

The elevator seems to be the focus for much of the supernatural activity. Whenever the last person is leaving for the day, she often hears the elevator go up and down a few times. Ms. San Angelo describes the ghost as lonely. "It's like he's saying, 'Don't go! Don't go!' I've experienced that many times. Also, he greets you, if you're the first person to arrive in the morning, by opening the elevator door as you approach it; that's happened to me as well."

At first, calls to the elevator company were placed, and their service people spent a year trying to explain and repair the odd behavior. No matter what they did, however, the activity continued on. The motor has been rebuilt three times, a new jack has been installed, and over the course of the years, most working parts have been replaced here and there. Still, the elevator activity continues. "When they couldn't find any explanation for the elevator's behavior," Ms. San Angelo said, "we jokingly started saying 'Maybe we have a ghost!'" Once that explanation was raised, though, things started falling into place. Because the spirit seemed to be fascinated with the elevator, the people in the building started calling him "Otis," after the name of the elevator company.

The Sammons Center serves as the home for twelve arts organizations representing every performing arts discipline, from the Shakespeare Festival of Dallas to the Turtle Creek Chorale. Over forty other arts organizations also regularly use the Center's services and facilities for rehearsals, meetings, performances, auditions, and special events. A few old-timers still remember the old pump station days, however. Once the building was in full operation, elderly gentlemen who had worked at the place back in its

The elevator, which seems to focus its attention on pretty, young ladies

Turtle Creek Pump Station days occasionally stopped by just to see the building again. Ms. San Angelo always tried to make a point of visiting with them, and she found that a few had a very interesting tale. It seems a young man in his early twenties had been killed in an accident at the station, and from that point on one particular part of the basement seemed to have a perpetual chill. Most of the workers avoided that area, feeling something just wasn't right there.

The fact that the elevator pit is the only remaining part of the basement may explain some of the activity there, along with another trait that is often displayed: When an attractive young girl in her early twenties walks by the elevator, no matter what time of day or who's in the building, the door will sometimes open automatically, as if some unseen doorman is welcoming her inside.

The behavior of the elevator alone would be fascinating enough, but on a few occasions the spirit has actually appeared to ladies who work in the building. He is described as a young man, wearing plain clothing, a jacket, and a workman's cap with a bill.

One such instance occurred when a woman was working at her desk in a first-floor office, and she looked up to see the man standing a few feet from her. "I'll be right with you," she said and briefly turned away. When she glanced back in the man's direction, he had vanished. It then occurred to her that it was still very early, long before normal hours, and the building was supposed to be locked. She got up to investigate and found that not only was the door to her office locked, but the front door to the building was secured as well. The lady went as far as to walk outside and check the parking lot, but there was no sign of anyone there. As Ms. San Angelo showed me the building, we passed a historical presentation area for the Dallas Water Utilities, and one photograph showed a few men standing on the floor of the pump station. She pointed to one man's hat, and said, "The ghost was wearing one kind of like that."

The spirit seems to have an affinity for people who work in the building during off-hours, and several years ago he apparently had a crush on one particular young lady, since he was always giving her attention. Reports she was working on would suddenly disappear from her computer, only to reappear the next day, as if someone was teasing her. On one occasion she was playing an instrumental CD in her office, and as she worked at her desk she realized that someone was singing along with the music. The song ended, and she heard laughter. The woman ejected the CD and took it to the gentleman in the next office, who played it from start to finish. There was no singing or laughter on the recording. The lady would often bring her dog to work, and while he was in her office, the dog would sit, stare at the corner, and bark at something unseen there.

The spirit pays most of his attention to the ladies—men haven't seen the ghost but have experienced the elevator going active as they lock up in the evening and the door opening when they arrive in the morning. One encounter between a male and the spirit did occur one evening, however. A maintenance worker who usually stayed late was in the kitchen on the second floor, getting ready to leave. He heard a voice outside of the kitchen door say, "Bye!" The worker automatically responded "Bye!" in return,

A hallway in one of the offices where the ghost has been seen

then he suddenly realized he was supposed to be alone in the building. He quickly checked the outside doors, and they were all locked tightly; he was the only one there.

In the past, Meadows Hall in the center was rented out for wedding receptions, and I remember attending one there. I mentioned that to Ms. San Angelo as we passed through the huge room, and she just smiled and said, "Back when we rented this room out to the public, Otis probably loved those receptions, with all the people laughing and having a good time in the building. I think he just gets lonely when the place is empty."

Perhaps he does, although with its many offices and rehearsal halls, Otis probably gets his share of companionship. I'll bet he is especially happy on jazz nights. The Sammons Center hosts *Sammons Jazz* each fall and spring, the only regular ongoing jazz performance series in the Dallas-Fort Worth area that features local jazz musicians. The tickets are very reasonably priced and include complimentary beer, wine, soft drinks, appetizers, and valet parking. The concerts often sell out, a fact that I'm sure makes Otis smile. I highly recommend taking in an evening of jazz there at the Sammons Center. If you go there, be sure to walk past the elevator, just to see what happens. If the door slides mysteriously open, it may just be that Otis wants to say "Hello."

> Historical Marker: Turtle Creek Pump Station
>
> Constructed in 1909 as a 15 million gallons per day primary pumping station for the city water supply. This brick industrial building was designed by Dallas Architect C. A. Gill. Its location on high ground afforded protection from floods that had damaged earlier stations. The building features ornate masonry detailing in the Italianate style. Last used as a pump station in 1930, the structure is a symbol of Dallas' growth at the turn of the century. Recorded Texas Historic Landmark 1983

Sammons Center for the Arts
3630 Harry Hines Blvd.
Dallas, TX 75219
Phone: 214.520.7788
Web: http://www.sammonsartcenter.org/

# The Phantom Shoppers of Olla Podrida

Head southward on Coit Road off of I-635 North, and you will see a large building on the west side with a rainbow-colored sign "Olla Podrida." The building's marquis currently reads, "Closed. Thanks for 24 great years." Unfortunately, the unique shopping village has permanently shut its doors. When the shop owners at Olla Podrida said goodbye to each other a final time and walked out the front door, though, many knew that the building would never quite be empty.

　　When it opened in 1972, Olla Podrida was a Nirvana for local shoppers and tourists alike. It was a specialty center for arts and crafts, boasting many galleries and showplaces, a full-service post

office, and even a theater. Shoppers could find HO-scale trains, dollhouse furniture, exquisite paintings, sculptures, and more at Olla Podrida. Several jewelry stores attracted a daily crowd, and the fast food was even worth waiting for. At night, though, when the crowds thinned and the merchants were left alone, a supernatural side to the building arose.

Originally the structure was an airplane hangar on the far north outskirts of the city of Dallas. As the city grew, however, and enveloped the land around the hangar, the owners had to take a new approach to their property. In 1972 it was renovated to include four floors of shop space, although the many stairways and landings seemed to give the building the illusions of much, much more. But the architecture of the place isn't the only interesting thing about Olla Podrida

When the crowds quieted every day, an occasional smattering of footsteps could be heard on the stairways and in the halls. The crafts persons who were working late would look up to glimpse a family dressed in turn-of-the-century clothing passing by. Those curious enough to step outside of their shop would find that the hallways were empty—the family of a man, his wife, and their daughters had disappeared. One lingering, tangible bit of evidence was the cigar smoke from the husband's stogie. That, and the laughter of his youngest daughter that seemed to echo though Olla Podrida in the late evening hours.

Jake Jegelewicz, owner of Jake's - the Unique, the Unusual, the Exotic in Olla Podrida, remembers the stories of the ghosts. "I did scrimshaw, silverwork, scratchboard, poetry, and some Native American tools and weapons," Jake explained. "I spent some nights working late and although I never really had an *experience,* there were times I did feel as though there was someone else around!"

He also remembers the wonderful camaraderie among the shop owners. Jake told me if I ran into any other merchants, "Tell them I said Hi. They will remember me as the guy who chained his Harley to a tree out back!"

Along with the shops in Olla Podrida, there was also a theater that was one of the hotspots in Dallas. Entertainers who played there include Roddy McDowall, the Kingston Trio, John Goodman, Douglas Fairbanks Jr., and Ray Charles. When the lights went down nightly at Granny's Dinner Playhouse, another spirit was often seen—a woman in dark clothing who seemed to be a sad, somber presence. There was no explanation as to who it might be, nor did the lady ever give any clues to her identity.

On July 31, 1996, the doors to Olla Podrida were locked to the public for the last time. The people who worked there had no doubt about the presence of the spirits, so the question that now remains is: what will become of them? The lady in black and the ghostly family who was responsible for the children's laughter and the pungent cigar smoke of the father—are their lonely spirits still wandering the building? Who can say? One twist to this story is that the property has been donated to a private school, which will be building new classrooms and offices in the near future. Perhaps the ghosts of Olla Podrida will have a new home, and a never-ending source of human accompaniment as the students roll through year after year. I believe that a year or so after the school opens, I'll have to pay it a visit to chat with a teacher or two. You never know, maybe they will have caught the image of a family walking through the halls out of the corner of their eye, heard the mysterious laughter of children, and smelled an old cigar.

Olla Podrida (now closed)
12215 Coit Rd.
Dallas, TX 75251

# A Ghost Among the Flowers

One of the most relaxing things to do in the city is to visit the Dallas Arboretum and Botanical Gardens. It's right beside White Rock Lake. When you visit, you'll find plush lawns, beautiful gardens, and grand old trees landscaped in breathtaking splendor.

From the descriptions, you might guess that I'm not a stranger to the place, and you'd be correct. One of the best things about it is that the Arboretum is a year-round attraction; you can visit to see the new blooms in spring, and then come right back a few months later to enjoy the beautiful fall colors. It's a wonderful place to spend a relaxing, romantic afternoon strolling through the gardens.

It's easy to walk through the Arboretum and imagine that it's been there forever, but in fact, it really hasn't. The whole idea started with a gentleman named Everette DeGolyer many years ago, who wanted to establish an arboretum for the city. A millionaire oilman, geologist, and philanthropist, he chaired a committee to find a location for the gardens, and although it was never realized during his lifetime, he'd probably be very pleased to know that the final property selection was his own estate...even though the decision was made many years later.

The Dallas Arboretum and Botanical Society incorporated in 1974 and after getting organized, raised the money necessary to transform the DeGolyer Estate into the botanical garden that it is today—at least, the beginnings of it. The estate had been purchased from Southern Methodist University by the city of Dallas, for the express purpose of a city arboretum.

One of the many flower-lined paths at the Arboretum

By 1980 the Society had raised the awareness of the Arboretum and had enlisted the support of Dallas businesses and civic organizations. Their funds grew to over one million dollars and enabled the purchase of the Camp Estate, which was located next door to the former Degolyer Estate and looked out over beautiful White Rock Lake.

In 2000 the *Fort Worth Star-Telegram* gave the account of a docent at the 21,000-square-foot Spanish mission style mansion that was once the home of Everette L. DeGolyer and his wife, Nell Goodrich DeGolyer. The docent's story is the only one I found of a ghost there, and in fact, the people I asked seemed confused that I would even pose the question of such things.

The docent, however, was convinced that something supernatural had taken place in the palatial old home. She had done her preparations for the job, memorizing pages worth of historical information, following the experienced docents through their paces to learn the job, and finally becoming a tour guide on her own.

The DeGolyer mansion

The Dallas Arboretum is open until five o'clock every day of the year, later in the summer, and even later for special occasions. It was one such event that found the young docent at the DeGolyer mansion very late in the evening. In fact, the building had been locked up for the night, but when she realized that she'd left her keys inside, she had to find a security guard to accompany her back to the home. He let her back into the building and waited by the door while she began a search for the missing keys.

The docent remembered putting them down on a desk in the office, but of course, they weren't where she remembered laying them. The house was deserted and quiet, and as she dug under piles of paper, she heard noises coming from deep inside the house. Recalling that she couldn't "distinguish it as a voice or music or anything specific," the young lady continued her search.

The noise came again, though, so she decided to investigate. Walking through the bedroom, then the dark hallway, nothing seemed to be out of place. With her docent training in the back of her mind, she knew that she'd need to check everything out. In her words, "I crossed the hall and got chills the instant I set foot into the living room entrance. Through the slight light coming in from the window, I was able to feel my way to a floor lamp near the doorway. I was shaking and sweating. I was so nervous, there would have been no way I could have gone in if that lamp had been an inch farther into the room. Turning on the lamp, I saw that the piano in the corner of the room, just under Mrs. DeGolyer's portrait, had the lid propped up like it was ready to be played." A photo of Mr. DeGolyer usually sat on top of the piano's lid, but that evening it had been moved to the gate leg table in front of a window not far from the piano." The unnerving thing to the docent was that the piano had not been open earlier. "I am *certain* it was not like that as we left at 5:30 when the house closed!" she said.

The piano, with Mr. DeGolyer's photo on top

There was an eerie feeling in the room, but the docent was determined to set things right before leaving. "I took a few determined steps forward to close the piano and replace the photo, but as I got closer, for some reason I felt I shouldn't. I turned and ran, leaving the photo where it was. When I got back to the office, I pushed the papers aside, no longer caring about the semi-organization, grabbed the keys, and slammed the door after me."

Even though the girl was frightened, she had the presence of mind to plan to be the first one to unlock the doors the next day, so that anything she'd found out of place that evening could be corrected in the morning light, before anyone else arrived.

And arrive early she did. "I nearly screamed when I saw that the piano lid was down and the photo was back in its place on top. I was so freaked out, I said I was sick and left and didn't work the next three days. Later I felt better about it and actually started thinking the idea there might be a ghost."

She was never able to find anyone else who'd had a supernatural experience in the home, but that didn't change what she'd seen with her own eyes—the piano had been opened, as if someone had been preparing to play a nocturnal concerto among the flowers there at the Arboretum.

Dallas Arboretum
8525 Garland Road
Dallas, TX 75218
Phone: 214.327.8263
Event hotline: 214.327.4901
Web: http://www.DallasArboretum.org


# The Spirits of the Sons of Hermann Hall

The Sons of Hermann Hall is an institution in the Deep Ellum section of Dallas. It is best known as a venue for musicians, and many recognized artists have played there. The hall has even been used by singers like Robert Earl Keen and Ed Burleson to record live albums. Personally, I remember seeing great performers like Guy Clark and Gary P. Nunn at the hall in past years. All that, and I never knew the place was haunted!

When I heard about the ghost in the hall, I put my researcher hat on and dove right in. My first question was: Who the heck is Hermann?!? With a little digging, I was able to find out that he was

a Germanic folk hero named Hermann the Cherusker. Now, this has absolutely nothing to do with the haunting, but it was interesting enough that I just have to pass it on.

As it turns out, Webster's Biographical Dictionary included Hermann, but under a name that the Romans gave him when he was captured: Arminius. But I'm getting ahead of myself.

When the armies of Rome overran Germany, many prisoners were taken, and Hermann was one of them. The Romans recognized his military potential, gave him the Roman name of Arminius, and forced him to become a Legionnaire. He quickly rose through the ranks to become a decorated leader and was a darling of the Empire. Hermann began to notice the cruelty and oppression that his former countrymen received from Rome, though, and decided it was up to him to make a stand. He organized the men from the German tribes into a military unit to challenge the three Roman legions that were occupying the countryside at the time. In the Battle of Teutoberger Forest, which took place in A.D. 9, the forces led by Hermann soundly thrashed the Romans. He was twenty-seven years old at the time.

There was a price for his heroics, however. The Romans kidnapped his wife, who was pregnant with his son, and took her away to Rome, never to be seen by Hermann again. Our hero died twelve years later, but his bravery has been remembered in song and legend ever since. Monuments to the Germanic hero stand in Detmold, Germany; New Ulm, Minnesota; and, oddly enough, in the German village at Six Flags Fiesta Texas in San Antonio.

In New York City, back in 1840, a group of men of Germanic descent decided to form a fraternal organization. Looking back at the history of their ancestors' homeland, they learned about the brave warrior Hermann, and the Sons of Hermann organization was born.

Trust me, we're getting to the ghosts. I just want to finish out the tie between the organization in New York and the historic old hall in Dallas. With that in mind, I'll simply say that by 1847 there were 800 members in the lodge in six northern states. As settlers migrated to Texas, many of those in the Texas Hill Country were of German descent. They established towns such as Fredricksburg and New Braunfels and brought with them a wonderful slice of Germanic culture.

The Sons of Hermann, with its Germanic roots, soon found its way into these settlements and began to spread across the state. The Dallas Lodge (#22) was chartered in 1890, and the Columbia Lodge (#60) was chartered in 1893. In 1910 the lodges combined and built a meeting hall at 3414 Elm Street, which is the Sons of Hermann Hall that has come to be an integral part of the Deep Ellum community.

Armed with all that history, I decided to head down to the Hall about 5:30 in the evening. There was a band playing there later, and I knew the place would be packed by then, so I was hoping I'd beat the crowd.

I parked my car across the street and walked through the front door, as I had done several times in the past. One note of warning about Deep Ellum: The tow trucks circle the area like vultures, and if you park illegally, you'll be towed before you can even get your car locked!

Walking down the hall, I saw the bar to my right and figured that would be the best place to start out. There were a few people sitting there watching television, including the bartender. I'd walked into something very special. It was like I'd joined a bunch of friends at a neighborhood watering hole. The bartender greeted me, I explained what I was doing there, and he came right over and started telling me about the Sons of Hermann Hall.

Staircase where children's voices were heard

"Oh, there's always something happening." He pointed out of the doorway toward the beautiful wooden staircase. "We were down here in a meeting one night, when we heard a bunch of kids laughing and playing on those stairs." He paused, smiled, and shook his head. "'Course when we looked, there was no one there. No children were in the hall that night."

One of the people sitting at the bar piped up about then. "Tell him about your dad and the light upstairs!"

The bartender picked the tale right up. "Yep, my father used to work here, and he was the last one to leave one night. Just like he always did, he locked everything up tight then walked out to his car and started driving away. He happened to glance back, and just as he did, the upstairs light snapped on." The fellow stopped to let that sink in a minute. "Now, there was no doubt that he'd been the last person in the hall. Of course, he turned the car around and went back. The door was still locked, and by the time my father unlocked it and ran upstairs, the light was off again. He looked around just to make sure, but there wasn't another person in the place."

The upstairs hall—scene of real-world concerts and ghostly activity

I was enthralled, listening to the gentleman talk. I finally asked him if he'd seen any of these things. He shrugged his shoulders. "There's lots of people around here who could tell you lots of stories. I'm one of them." He pointed in various directions around the room. "There always a door over here, or over there, that's acting up. Doors that we leave open close by themselves, and ones that we close end up being open next time you look." He lowered his voice and leaned in toward me. "And some of them were even locked."

"I even saw someone once. I was working upstairs, early, before anyone else got here. A fellow walked past, and it startled me, because I knew I was alone. I turned my head to see who it was, and the man had vanished. He just wasn't there. Of course, I checked downstairs, and everything was still locked securely. I don't have an explanation as to what it could have been."

We talked a little more, and I asked if I could snap a few photos. He told me that I basically had the run of the place, so I went exploring on my own. I climbed the stairs, where the phantom children had been heard playing. Lining the walls were the photos and placards and memorabilia of the past performances. Truly impressive—it was like a mini-museum.

From there I walked into the empty hall upstairs that was used for concerts, my footsteps echoing through the large room. I have to tell you, in all sincerity, I felt like I wasn't in there alone. I can't say what it was, but something was there in the room. I walked from one corner to the other, snapped several photos, and finally made my way downstairs.

One of the guys from the bar had unlocked their four-lane bowling alley for me to see, and I had a chance to visit a little more. As we sat there, I asked if anything ever happened in the bar. The bartender cracked a smile and said, "Well, when we close up, after everyone's gone, we clean the place, stack all the dishes, and put the room back in order. Occasionally I'll open back up the next day, and everything is moved around in here. The things on the bar have been shuffled around, just like someone was in here after we locked the place. It's happened enough that I know there's no way anyone could have gotten into the building during the night. They just couldn't."

Since I was there that early, the bar was still in perfect order. Everything was in its place, clean and symmetrical, and I could only imagine how it must feel to unlock the front door and find everything disheveled and in complete disarray.

After listening to the gentleman behind the bar speak, I had no doubt in my mind there were spirits wandering the corridors of the Sons of Hermann Hall. And seeing the place brought back a lot of memories. I'd been to see many performers there over the last couple of decades. The next time I come back, though, I'll be looking at things a little differently, now that I know what goes on there when the place is quiet. I'll definitely show up early to have a frosty beverage in the bar with the good folks there, and I'm going to have to have one of the burgers from Chilo's Kitchen downstairs that I've heard so much about. That, and I'm anxious to walk back into the performance hall upstairs, just to see if the same strange feeling comes over me when I stroll around inside. I have to tell you, there was something there with me.

Sons of Hermann Hall
3414 Elm Street (at Exposition)
Dallas, TX 75226-1720
Phone: 214.747.4422
Web: http://www.sonsofhermann.com

# The Mysterious Majestic Theatre

So why is the Majestic Theatre so mysterious? Well basically, because of all the mixed signals that I found while tracking down any ghosts there.

I've been attending performances at the Majestic Theatre for over a decade now, and I have to say, if any place should be haunted, it's the Majestic. Every wall inside is lavishly papered or draped, there are enough doorways, balconies, and passageways to make the Phantom of the Opera at home, and above all, the place has a very rich history.

You'll find it at 1925 Elm Street in downtown Dallas, although Elm has changed considerably since its construction. The theater was originally built by Karl Hoblitzelle, who traveled to Texas to make his fortune in the entertainment business. He hired

architect John Eberson of Chicago to build a magnificent showplace for the arts. Not only would the theater host motion pictures, but it was also the home to live theater and vaudeville acts.

The grand opening of the five-story Majestic was one big hoopla, held on April 11, 1921, complete with all the trappings: spotlights, limousines, and celebrities. The press immediately heralded it as the finest theater in all the world. The top-name performers from across the country brought their Vaudeville acts to the theater, including Mae West, Jack Benny, Milton Berle, George Burns and Gracie Allen, and even Bob Hope. Magicians who mystified audiences found the place to be a perfect venue: Houdini, Harry Blackstone, and Howard Thurston, along with many others, worked their magic in downtown Dallas.

Of course, getting a babysitter was as big a problem back then as it is today, but the theater had a perfect answer. If a patron had children, there was no need for a sitter; the kids were welcome to just come along! A nursery called "Majesticland" was provided for the kids. It was a child's dream, a fantasy world complete with a petting zoo and a carousel.

Even as the Majestic rode the crest of the wave, things began to slow down for the grand old dame of Elm Street. Vaudeville was soon passé with the masses, and the world became infatuated with the new invention of talking pictures. The theater management knew they had to change with the times, so the Majestic became almost exclusively a movie house. Not content to be an ordinary motion picture theater, though, the Majestic became the home to many premiers. Movies that made their debut there featured the top stars of the day: Gregory Peck, Jimmy Stewart, and "The Duke," John Wayne.

When motion pictures weren't being screened, live entertainment was still brought into the theater. During the "Big Band" era, stars such as Cab Calloway and Duke Ellington played there with their orchestras.

Cinemaplexes began to rise in the surrounding suburbs, however, and the crowds waned in downtown Dallas. On July 16, 1973, the Majestic Theatre closed its doors, going dark after its final showing of the James Bond film *Live and Let Die*. For all intents and purposes, the theater had taken its last breath.

With such a history as all that, you'd think the place might very well have acquired a spirit or two over the years, and perhaps it had.

In 1976 the Majestic Theatre was given to the city of Dallas, and the Oglesby Group served as architects for the renovation of the historic old building. The theater became the first Dallas building to be listed on the prestigious National Register of Historic Places in 1977, and in 1983 it was awarded a Texas Historical Commission Marker.

Today the theater hosts national-caliber performances of musicals and Broadway plays in the guise of the Dallas Summer Musicals and the Dallas Broadway Series. Personally, I've seen performers such as Joan Collins, Judd Hirsch, and David Copperfield there. Every time I walk through those doors, it's hard not to just stop and soak in all the ambiance of the place. I never cease to be impressed by its majesty.

But what about the ghosts?

Well, in the writing of this book, I contacted the Majestic Theatre personnel and was summarily told that the theater was not haunted and that whatever ghost stories I might have heard were not true. To be completely honest, I was directly informed that the current regime would not perpetuate the lies of any ghosts in the theater. A little harsh, but I just let it pass. After all, I was told they give the same story to *The Dallas Morning News* when they call every October for a Halloween article.

Ordinarily, that would have been enough for me to scrap any mention of the theater in this book. I wouldn't want to waste my time doing any more digging on the subject, nor would I want to take you, the reader, through anything that wasn't going to be at least somewhat interesting. As they say, though, a funny thing happened one day....

I was doing research for another haunted location in North Texas and ran across an article in *The Dallas Morning News* from October 31, 1999. A reporter named Catherine Cuellar had filed a story about a few places around town that had ghost stories, and the Majestic Theatre was one of the properties included.

Not only was the theater featured in the article, but Ronnie Jessie, the program coordinator for the Majestic Theatre at the time, described an event that was a little unnerving. A security guard was making his normal rounds in the theater one evening. As he passed the stage, a backdrop began to slowly descend onto to the stage, as if on cue. Other than that, the theater was quiet and empty. According to Mr. Jessie, the guard called out the names of the other people in the building, but there was no answer. Even though he was completely alone, the backdrop just continued to unroll. But it wasn't some electrical malfunction or mechanical failure. "You have to crank this by hand to let the backdrop down," Mr. Jessie told *The Dallas Morning News*. Had the backdrop mechanism slipped, it would have unrolled very quickly and spilled down onto the stage. There was just no explanation as to how it could glide down, as if some unseen hand was slowly unrolling the backdrop. The guard explored the stage area, and when he could find no one there, he manually cranked the backdrop back up.

The former managing director for the theater, Celia Barshop, also gave her version of a ghost story in the article, speaking about working alone in the building early one Saturday morning. "I smelled this fabulous aroma of cooking food. I walked into the commercial kitchen on the second floor, but there was no smell." She looked around to find that all the doors were locked and the lights were off. No one had been cooking in the place, yet the smell wafted throughout the theater. In the main lobby, Ms. Barshop was overwhelmed by what she described as the scent of Sunday brunch, which was stronger and more enticing than the first odors.

She went back to the kitchen, and although there was still no one inside, it felt to her as if she was not alone. Ms. Barshop wedged a wooden stop under the door to hold it open while she tried to determine the source of the enticing smell. She searched the refrigerators, ovens, and trashcans, but there was nothing to indicate that any food had been prepared there. Even the burners on the stove were cold—the kitchen had not been used. She turned around to go back to her office and saw that the door she had propped open had somehow been closed.

She turned back to the empty room and said, "Enjoy your meal. Please don't cause me any harm. I won't bother you."

After the experience, Ms. Barshop told *The Dallas Morning News*, "I'm sure there's some logical explanation, but I believe in ghosts."

There are many such stories from people who worked there, all willing to use their names and tell their individual tales. The Office of Cultural Affairs staff even took to calling the supposed ghost "Mr. Hoblitzelle," after the man who originally built the place. A portrait of Karl Hoblitzelle hangs in the fifth-floor conference room of the theater, and people swear that his eyes follow them as they move around the room.

Could it be the spirit of old Karl knocking around the theater? Or were they—as I was told during my phone call—lies by the former regime to attract publicity?

This is the mystery of the Majestic Theatre. It could well be that the employees from the past were correct in their descriptions of the spirits that reside in the old building. On the other hand, the current theater management could be correct that there is absolutely no ghostly activity in the theater at all.

But it can't be both ways.

I don't know. I really don't. All I can say is I love that old place, and every time I go there, I'll be keeping my eyes open for any supernatural presence moving around with the crowds.

If I ever do a sequel to this book down the road, maybe I'll contact the theater management once again—whoever they happen to be at the time—just to see what they say. Perhaps the story will have changed a bit, as more and more time has passed and the spirits of the theater have made themselves known once again.

All I know for sure is that the Majestic Theatre is a very, very mysterious place, indeed.

The Majestic Theatre
1925 Elm St.
Dallas, TX 75201
Phone: 214.880.0137
Web: http://www.dallassummermusicals.org

# The Ghosts of Denton

When I arrived in Denton in my journeys for this book, I realized I was once again at a county seat. They just kept cropping up in my travels. This city was much different from most of the others, however, in that it is very young by comparison. In fact it was founded in 1857 for the sole purpose of being the county seat, and the land was chosen because of the central location. Three landowners donated about one hundred acres for the town, and city planners began to lay it out for settlement. It assumed the same name as its county, which was named for John B. Denton, an early settler in North Texas who was mentioned in the "Bird's Fort" story in this book.

Despite the fact that the city began to accumulate businesses such as mills, blacksmiths, groceries, and light manufacturing, one of the things that set it apart from other towns in the area was the establishment of North Texas Normal College in 1890, which would become the University of North Texas today. Now, I've been to several writers' conferences at UNT, never guessing that it began so long ago and contributed so much to the history of Denton. Both of the haunted locations I found there were on the UNT campus, in fact, and I had a great time tracking them both down.

There were a couple of other places in Denton rumored to be haunted—Argyle Bridge and the old hospital. The bridge has a legend where automatic car door locks are supposed to go off by themselves when you drive over. I drove over many bridges while looking for Argyle, and the door locks didn't misbehave in my car at all. Since I couldn't find any credible sources who'd had anything happen on the bridge, I just left the story alone. The old hospital had a more elaborate tale, one where a nurse had an affair with a married doctor, as the story goes, and died in an attempt to rid herself of his baby. She supposedly continued to appear to the staff and the patients there, but I could find nothing more than the legend, so it went by the wayside as well. Besides, they were nothing compared to the ghosts that haunt the two dorms on UNT campus, whose presence seem to be detected on a regular basis!

# The Attic Ghost of Bruce Hall

You've heard of people who are "professional students." They work on degree after degree, never seeming to want to leave college. Well, a young lady at the University of North Texas may have taken that concept to the next level. You see, Bruce Hall has a spirit of a young college girl who has lingered there for decades!

I first heard about the ghost of Bruce Hall from a friend of mine who went to UNT. I was inquiring about any spirits in Denton, and he said, "Well, there's the music dorm on campus. That's supposed to have a ghost or two." Armed with that small bit of information, I started digging into information on the university itself. I found a dormitory located next to the Music Building, a popular residence for UNT's students of fine arts, that had a tale or two about ghosts: Bruce Hall.

With a little more digging, I was able to uncover the fact that the building has quite an impressive history. It was opened in 1948 as a residential hall for the university, named after Dr. William Herschel Bruce, Ph.D. Dr. Bruce died in 1943 at the age of 87 years. He was named as the third president of North Texas in 1906 and served until 1923, when he elected to resign in order to attend his ailing wife. Dr. Bruce was a favorite with the students, staff, and the university officials, and therefore the Board of Regents accepted his resignation with both disappointment and understanding. The board wanted to keep Dr. Bruce involved with the school, however, so they unanimously elected him President Emeritus and Professor of Education. During his association with the university, North Texas grew from a small college with a few

Entrance to Bruce Hall

buildings into a highly respected graduate institution with flourishing educational programs. To honor the memory of Dr. Bruce after his death, the university assigned his name to a huge residential hall that was being planned.

When I started asking around about Bruce Hall, I quickly learned there was something special about the people who lived there. They dub themselves "Brucelings" and are a rowdy, lively, caring bunch—a family, really, not a collection of building-dwellers who happen to co-reside. They laugh and play together. There are resident concerts and debates in the lobby and impromptu jam sessions throughout the hall. All that, and a ghost or two keeping everyone company.

Stop and ask anyone in the common area about their ghosts, and they'll say something like, "Oh, you mean Wanda!" Everyone knows about her, although she seems to be a little private in her existence in the building. Few have seen her or felt her presence, but the lady's legacy lives on. I heard several stories, but the one most people agreed on is that Wanda was a resident who lived in the hall in the 1950s, in the first decade of the building's existence.

I was searching for someone who knew some of the specific details about Wanda, but I hit a jackpot with amateur paranormal investigator Stephen Barnett. Steve is also the drummer for Baboon, a band formed in Denton while he was a student at the University of North Texas and Bruce Hall resident. Steve gives a classic version of the Wanda story: "Well, as legend has it, she was a girl who lived in the dorm many years ago, in the fifties, I think. Apparently she had become pregnant but was too ashamed to admit it to anyone, so she decided to hide her condition from her friends and family. Months went by, and she kept up the pretense of being just another student until her secret became too obvious to conceal, and here's where the story gets creepy. She must have gone off the deep end at this point, because she snuck into the Bruce Hall attic and hid there, day in and day out, for who knows how long. Eventually she gave birth to her baby, put him in a cardboard box, and left him there. When Wanda's body was eventually found, she was sitting in the attic, in a chair facing a solitary window overlooking the campus grounds. Her baby, also dead, lay in the box by her side. And to this day people claim to see a young woman's silhouette in the window, late on moonlit nights, peering into the darkness."

Creepy enough, but that was only the beginning for Stephen. He goes on to say, "I happened to be friends with a few of the resident assistants at Bruce, and I began to ask questions. Turns out there were all kinds of stories about Wanda. For instance, students living on the top floor of the dorm would often complain of noises coming from the attic—footsteps, voices, and heavy dragging sounds. A resident advisor—an R.A.—also told me that Wanda became particularly active when there were no students around, such as over holidays or breaks. He said that he knew a girl who freaked out one time. The R.A.s were all at Bruce Hall over a break, and one of their duties was to check each of the wings every day to make sure nobody was messing around. One girl was checking wings and something happened to her. She was found standing in one of the shower stalls with her clothes on, crying. It was pretty weird, and she wouldn't talk about it. Another incident happened when an R.A. was checking the rooms, and when he stuck his head into one in particular, the blinds in the window suddenly fell. That sort of scared him, but he didn't think anything of it and continued to the next room. When he looked through the next doorway, though, the blinds in that room fell down too. Terrified, he began to run down the hall, and each door he passed— VRRRPPP!!!—the blinds fell down. The guy said when he was running it was like something was brushing against his ear, like somebody was touching him. Another time, a fellow was doing his rounds and he saw a girl standing in the hall. He shouted at her, you know, 'Hey! What are you doing here?' but she turned and went around the corner. So he runs down the hall after her, and when he gets around the corner she's not there anymore. It was a dead end. She was just gone."

Those accounts given to Stephen only fueled the fire, however, so he arranged to have himself locked in the attic of Bruce Hall, the very place where Wanda died, to see for himself what might be there. With an R.A. as an accomplice and armed with a camcorder and flashlight, Stephen entered the attic at midnight. As he recalls, "The door to the attic looked every bit as creepy as any door could—big and bulky, slightly crooked and with big mysterious gashes across the front. My R.A. friend unlocked the door and let it swing open then asked me if I was sure I wanted to go through with it. I stepped inside and immediately noticed a slight draft. It was completely dark, aside from the meager amount of light that streamed in from the window, and in the distance, I could just barely make out the form of a chair silhouetted there."

He'd taken his own chair in so as not to disturb the one that was reportedly Wanda's, so Stephen began his trek through the attic. "The door closed and I heard my friend lock it from the other side. I spent a few seconds in the blackness before I managed to get the flashlight switched on, and then I turned towards the narrow walkway. If I took a wrong step, I'd fall through the insulation and come crashing down into one of the rooms. As I dragged my chair along, slowly negotiating the crossbeams in the dark, I occasionally heard the rafters rattle, whereupon I swung my flashlight around to take a look. Of course, there was nothing there and I assumed that either my steps or the wind had caused the noise, or maybe it was the sound of my friend downstairs, doing his rounds. I kept moving, regardless. As I stepped up to the chair in the attic, I switched on the camcorder and positioned my own chair in front of hers. 'Wanda?' I whispered. I sat down and shined my flashlight at the empty chair in front of me. A very creepy moment. I could imagine turning off the flashlight, calling her name, turning the light back on, and there she'd be—a ghastly fright-mask poised to munch on my brain. So naturally, that seemed the right thing to do, and I turned off the flashlight. Quiet and black."

Sitting there in the dark, Stephen rolled tape with the camcorder and would occasionally call her name to see if the spirit would make an appearance that night. But every time he switched the flashlight back on, Wanda's chair was empty. Stephen wasn't ready to give up, though: "I asked Wanda, 'Can you give me some sort of a sign?' Twenty minutes later I heard the attic door open, and there was my friend. I picked up my chair and made my way back. I assumed it was over.

"Back in my room with my friends, I plugged the camera into our VCR and rewound the tape. Something happened. My television suddenly, without any logical explanation, switched itself OFF. Let me make this clear—it had NEVER done that before. I immediately spun around and looked at my two friends, neither of whom seemed to be paying much attention, and then I checked for the remote. It was on my desk, at least 5 feet away from either of them. We all went pale, and my roommate shouted something about dying. Nothing unusual was on the videotape, but the experience was a memorable one nonetheless."

Does the spirit of Wanda walk the corridors of Bruce Hall? The residents there certainly seem to think so, and after all, they live with her on a daily basis.

University of North Texas
Bruce Hall
1624 Chestnut
Denton, TX 76203
Phone: 940.565.4343
Web: http://www.unt.edu/brucehall/

# Brenda's Spirit in ᥃aple Street ᥃all

As I was nosing around the University of North Texas, checking out leads on the ghost in Bruce Hall, I kept hearing there was another dorm on campus that was haunted—or at least had a few ghostly tales associated with it.

There were several false leads, and I chased them all. Believe me, trying to find a legitimate ghost story there on campus was driving me crazy. I was running into wall after wall. Everyone that I talked to seemed to have heard about some other ghosts on campus but just couldn't remember exactly which dorm they were in. I was getting frustrated.

Ah, but just like so many other times in my life, my wife came to my rescue. You see, she received a Masters from the University of North Texas several years ago and as an active alumnus, still receives *The North Texan*, a magazine that chronicles everything from new developments on campus to happenings with the graduates there. While wading through back issues, just to see what might turn up, I realized they also had an online version that might be easier to search. Sure enough, I discovered a jewel in the Winter 2001 issue of *The North Texan Online*! The Time Tracks section of the magazine had a Ghost Stories segment that quoted one of the former residents of Maple Street Hall, the second oldest dorm on campus, with a few spirited tales. This gave me hope, because if the oldest dorm, Bruce Hall, had its ghost, then surely the second oldest would have one of its own.

The ghost, although completely harmless, has manifested herself often enough that the residents have given her a name: Brenda. For many years, Maple Street Hall (or Maple Hall, as many people call it around campus) was an all-female dorm, so it follows that its apparition might therefore be the spirit of a young lady—and so it is.

Now, there are two different stories as to how the ghost came to be there. One is that a young girl who lived in the hall was the victim of a terribly violent crime and died not far away from her on-campus home of Maple Hall, which is why her spirit has chosen

94                                        *The Ghosts of Denton*

Maple Street Hall

to linger there. The other tale is remarkably similar to the Bruce Hall story, where a girl suffers the incredible embarrassment of the day of discovering that she is "with child" but decides to try to hide the condition. As the second story about the place goes, the girl died while giving birth to a child in some hidden area of Maple Street Hall. Now, while both of these accounts are suspicious as to their accuracy, one solid fact remains: a spirit is haunting Maple Street Hall.

According to *The North Texan*, a resident advisor was inspecting her wing before the students came in to start the fall semester in 1995, inventorying the rooms and documenting their conditions. As each room was completed, the light was turned out and the door shut. It was an easy way to tell which rooms had been completed and which rooms remained.

When the resident advisor had finished the rooms she was responsible for, she was completing a few final tasks when a telephone began to ring in one of the rooms in the wing. And since all the doors were closed, it had to be in one of the rooms she'd already inspected. Normally this wouldn't be an unusual occurrence, even though the students weren't there. Residents from the previous semester would have given their number out to many people, and some of those folks might still use it, not knowing it was a vacant dorm room. The phone didn't stop, however, and so the resident assistant set out to find the room and set the caller straight.

It wasn't long until she found the room where the phone was ringing, and as it turns out, it wasn't that hard to do. Unlike every other room, this one had the door open, and the light had been turned on, even though the resident assistant was the only person in the wing. When she walked through the door of the room, the ringing suddenly stopped, as if some spirit had lured her inside.

Totally panicked, she ran in a dead heat to another wing in the dorm to tell another advisor what was going on. That person just smiled and told her there was a simple explanation: The wing she was in charge of was haunted.

While there were many other things that happened during the course of that resident advisor's stay, one particular instance made quite an impression: a phantom suitemate.

Maple Street Hall does have a few rooms with private baths, but for the most part the bathrooms serve suites—basically, a few students. While it is still a community bathroom, the arrangement is much better than the dorms that have only one per floor! The same resident assistant from the previous incident had one empty room on her final semester there, but nevertheless, two students who were suitemates with the empty room came knocking on her door one day to ask who their neighbors were. The girls explained that they were anxious to meet their suitemates and therefore knocked on the door on several occasions, at all times of day, but no one was ever there. When the resident advisor told them the room was empty, the girls looked shocked and went on to explain that every morning someone had taken a shower in the bathroom before they got up, just as if someone was inhabiting the other suite.

The girls insisted that they had heard the water running during the phantom shower and after it cut off, had gone in to find the shower stall wet. It had every sign that a student had finished her shower there.

The resident advisor took them into the empty suite that shared their bathroom to prove there was no one residing there. After that, though, she moved students into the room as soon as possible, just to keep the balance of things. After all, a showering ghost would not only be wasting water, but would also be very unnerving to the other students in the hall!

University of North Texas
Maple Street Hall
1621 Maple St.
Denton, TX 76203

# The Ghosts of Fort Worth

**F**ort Worth is a special place to our family. My wife was born at All Saints Children's Hospital, and her mother as well as aunt and uncles grew up there. We have several family members who still live there, and so it is a city I tend to visit from time to time. Whether it's two-stepping at the White Elephant Saloon in the Stockyards, or taking a leisurely stroll through the Water Gardens, Fort Worth is a wonderful place to visit.

The city is rich in the history of the Old West. It was established as an actual fort (hence the name) in 1849 in an effort to protect the settlers in the area from the Indian attacks that were a constant threat. General William Jenkins Worth had proposed a line of ten forts to form an impenetrable line of defense. The ten forts were never completed, but Major Ripley S. Arnold did establish one at a superb location on the banks of the Trinity River. He named it after the general, and because of its stronghold position, it began to attract pioneers in search of a new home.

Fort Worth grew from there, especially as a stopover on the old Chisholm Trail. The "Hell's Half Acre" section of town flourished in its notoriety. We'll be looking at some of the spirits that remain there, from the former bordello that is now Greene Antiques, to the bathhouse that stood in the place of Del Frisco's Double Eagle Steak House.

Just north of the acre lies the Fort Worth Stockyards, a destination for cowboys and cattlemen alike, and a place where a few ghosts roam today. We'll also be visiting the plush Stockyards Hotel, the Spaghetti Warehouse, and more haunted locations there.

Rather than dwell on the city's history in this introduction, I believe I'd rather just jump right into the destinations themselves

and let them tell their own story, one that is the very essence of
this country's frontier.

# The Protective Spirit of the Texas White House

I think one of the most interesting things about ghosts is how individual they all are—just like each one of us, the living. I ran across
the story of one fascinating spirit at the Texas White House, a
magnificent bed and breakfast in Fort Worth. The trouble was I
didn't have a chance of experiencing the ghost myself—he only
shows up for the ladies!

That didn't prevent me from stopping by for a visit with
Grover McMains, however, who owns and operates the bed and
breakfast with his wife, Jamie. Mr. McMains suggests the spirit
that lingers in one of the bedrooms is that of the former owner, but
we'll get to Mr. Newkirk in a bit.

The structure is a huge, stately home that was originally built
in 1910 by a couple named Newkirk. The neighborhood was a
rather well-to-do area, dominated by doctors and lawyers,
although Mr. Newkirk was in the investment business.

A tight-knit family, the Newkirks raised four boys in the home.
As you can imagine, the great stock market crash of 1929 hit the
family hard—harder than their neighbors, in fact, because of the
nature of Mr. Newkirk's business. The four boys all took jobs to
help bring in money for the family. They managed to survive the
terrible times, and life in the house slowly returned to normal.

A little over a decade later, the United States entered World
War II, and the four Newkirk boys all enlisted to serve their country. All four thankfully returned back to the home then left one by
one to start families of their own. Two of the boys moved away
from Fort Worth, and two remained behind. One that stayed, Richard Newkirk, served as mayor of Fort Worth for a brief period.

The family home was still a gathering place for the growing
Newkirk clan, and it stayed with the family through the death of

Front view of the Texas White House

the parents. Mr. Newkirk passed away in the house, followed a few years later in 1967 by his wife.

The boys sold the house after the death of their mother, and it became a series of small businesses over the next twenty-odd years, although it was never changed structurally. Just before Mr. and Mrs. McMains purchased the house in 1994, it was a restaurant named "The Texas White House" so the McMainses decided to keep the name.

The house was closed for two years as they labored to convert it into a luxurious bed and breakfast. Although some modifications were made to the rear of the house, the architect overseeing the project was given an architectural award for designing an addition to the house without changing the original lines or architectural style.

In 1996 the Texas White House opened for business, catering mainly to businesspersons during the week and romantic getaways for couples on the weekends. The McMainses advertise bubble baths for two and carriage rides for their guests and say, "The true art of romance involves creativity. Let us know what you have in mind—we can help make it happen!" They are also located within a few minutes of the business and medical districts and almost all of the major cultural and entertainment attractions in the downtown area. As people began to discover their bed and breakfast, business flourished, with countless satisfied guests.

Upstairs, a few strange occurrences were starting to be reported by guests. Mr. McMains explains: "The very first episode occurred when a woman came down to breakfast one morning and said that during the night she had felt what would be a person lying down at your back, if you were on your side and your partner lay down beside you, back to back. She felt that. She thought, of course, that it was someone and it startled her. She didn't move, and she lay there thinking, 'what am I going to do,' 'what's going to happen', that sort of thing. After a few minutes, she decided to move, to turn over and find out who this person was and do something about it. As she went to whirl around, she felt it move off the bed. She sensed that it was a person moving away, but of course, nothing was there. As far as I know, that was the only episode the first time."

The woman had been staying alone in the Lone Star room, which was the master bedroom of the former owners, Mr. and Mrs. Newkirk.

The next event in the room was much more subtle. Another woman, again, also staying in the room alone, had called her husband to touch base since he hadn't accompanied her on the trip. During their conversation, the ceiling fan started to rotate. She told her husband how strange it was, but he didn't seem fazed—until she added that the light switch was still in the "off" position, which eliminated the chance of any electricity flowing to the device. With no discernable stirring of air in the room to cause the fan to turn, the only explanation was some type of electromagnetic charge present in the room that was affecting the fan—the kind that is sometimes reported when spirits are present. As she continued to talk to her husband, the fan stopped as mysteriously as it had started.

"These things don't happen all the time," Mr. McMains says. "The events have been spread out over the course of a few years.

The bedroom where Mr. Newkirk occasionally
makes his presence known

The Lone Star is the most masculine room we have, so it usually isn't one that women staying here alone would choose to reserve. Also, many couples stay in the room, and the ghost simply doesn't show up when a man is there."

The spirit made its presence known on a third occasion that was very similar to the first two occurrences. A woman staying alone in the room had just fallen asleep when she awoke to the feeling of someone lying down on the bed with their back to hers. This person also felt no fear associated with the event but was certainly curious as to what was going on. She reached over to turn on the light and felt the presence move off of the bed. When she turned the lamp on, of course, the room was empty. At that moment her cellular phone started beeping, ringing, and flashing its lights, as if every single function on it had been activated at once. The phone was plugged in to recharge across the room, and the woman said it had never done anything like that before—nor did it reoccur during the remainder of her stay.

The McMains found out about the last event in the Lone Star room when its occupant, a lady staying alone, came down for breakfast who had no way of knowing what had happened in the past. She was traveling with a group of women who were college friends, and they were staying at the bed and breakfast for the weekend. She said, "You didn't tell me there was someone else staying in my room." Mr. McMains was confused and asked her to elaborate. "The presence in my room!" she replied, and went on to tell her story. She had been out for the day and returned to the room to freshen up before going out that evening. Upon returning, she said there was something—or someone—in the room whose presence was so intense that she felt exactly where it was standing beside the bed. It wasn't threatening, nor were there any ill feelings about it, so she continued getting ready to leave. As she came out of the bathroom, it was immediately apparent that the presence had moved to the other side of the bed. She finished getting ready, left for dinner, and when she returned the presence was gone.

Because these experiences have all taken place in the Lone Star room, the former master bedroom of the house, it is certainly possible that the spirit of Mr. Newkirk returns from time to time to check in on things. There has never been any fear associated with the presence, and in fact, one of the women observed that it was a "nice ghost." And since he was a gentleman of the early 1900s, it is even likely that when he finds there is a woman staying alone in the room, he makes his presence known just to let them know he's watching out for them. After all, in his time, women didn't travel alone all that often!

The Texas White House Bed & Breakfast
1417 Eighth Avenue
Fort Worth, TX 76104
Phone: 817.923.3597
Toll Free: 800.279.6491
Fax: 817.923.0410
Email: stay@texaswhitehouse.com
Web: http://www.texaswhitehouse.com

# The Grieving Ghost of
# Barber's Bookstore

I believe in serendipity—I just have to! You see, I'd just begun researching this book, when I received an out-of-the-blue email from Dwight A. Greene about his haunted bookstore in Fort Worth. Mr. Greene was full of information, and after reading his email, I was so intrigued I just had to delve into his place a little further.

Dwight and Sheila Greene own Greene's Antiques and Barber's Books, both in the same building in downtown Fort Worth. The structure is almost 100 years old, built in 1908, and a portion of the old bookstore is a former hotel that was part of the red-light district of Fort Worth. If any building deserves to have a few spirits hanging around, this one certainly does. It is located on the outskirts of an area of Fort Worth that used to be known as "Hell's Half Acre" in the Wild West days of the city. The area was filled with saloons, gambling establishments, and houses of ill repute. Shootings and gunfights were commonplace at the time.

Mr. Greene said that the bookstore has its own notorious history: "I was told by a Fort Worth old-timer that the brothels of that era were restricted to upper-story hotels only. He told me about going to downtown Fort Worth and hanging out on the street below these establishments when he was a kid. Since the girls liked to flash passers-by to attract business, they didn't particularly want kids lounging about on the street below. He went on to say that was how they would get their soda pop money: The girls would toss them coins to go away!"

I visited the bookstore on a Wednesday afternoon, and Mr. Greene's mother was kind enough to take me all around the building and share some of the ghost stories with me—both those she's heard and those she has experienced herself. One of the first stops was the back staircase, which led directly up to the old hotel floor. The Adams Hotel, it was called, and it was one of the shady places that occupied Hell's Half Acre.

We stopped just before reaching the top of the stairs, and she pointed through the railing at the upper-floor level of the staircase. We could just peek through it from our position. My tour guide said, "It happened right here. This is where the shot came from." As it turned out, a father found out that not only did his daughter work at the hotel entertaining the cowboys passing through town, but that she had also fallen in love with one and was planning to run away with him. The father showed up just as the man was leaving her room—number 11, a corner room that was right in front of us.

The father pulled his gun and shot the man dead in the hallway of the hotel. The girl was grief-stricken over the loss of her beloved and took her own life right there in the little room.

Apparently the spirit of the young girl is one of the unearthly inhabitants that still reside in the hotel. A few years ago the small rooms of the upstairs hotel were rented out to individual merchants, much like the antique malls that you see around town. A woman who displayed antiques in room 11 had a shelf by the door on which she placed cups and saucers. She would often arrive in the morning to find that the cups and saucers had been pushed off

Looking up the stairs where footsteps have been heard,
and from where the shot was fired by the angry father

the shelf, and Mr. Greene's mother told me, "I don't think the spirit of the young girl wanted them there."

We walked around the circular hallway of the old hotel, and I tried to imagine what it must have looked like back then. At the present time, the entire floor is a book-lover's dream. Shelves are overflowing with volumes on every subject imaginable. I could have spent hours there! It wasn't hard to envision the hotel's past days, though, with piano music floating in the air, the sound of horses in the street below, and the inviting call of the unoccupied ladies.

It was quiet on the day I was there, although I enjoyed many stories about some of the goings-on in the old place. Heavy footsteps have been heard climbing the stair, and in fact, I was told that the former owner had to go up and check it out several times by himself. He'd be there alone in the store with all of the doors locked, and a clumping would resound from the stairs. Perhaps the father was climbing them as he did many years ago, phantom gun in hand, looking for the cowpoke who had caught the fancy of his daughter.

Books drop on the wooden floor as well, sending the loud thump ringing through the empty building. And when the upper floor is quiet, the sound of pages turning has been heard, as if ghostly hands were perusing some of the countless volumes.

The hotel hallway, with the girl's rooms on either side

As we threaded our way around shelves and stacks of books in the old hotel, Mr. Greene's mother stopped and turned around. In a low voice, she said, "I've felt her right here. There's a scent of musty perfume that you pick up when she's here. A lot of people have smelled it." Apparently the girl is still in the hotel, grieving for her love that she lost in the Old West Romeo and Juliet tale.

She then turned me around toward a shelf. "Others feel her pass by as they're looking at the books, just like this." She brushed the sleeve of my shirt with her hand, as if someone had gently bumped up against me in passing. "It's like that. Just a touch as she walks by. Of course, when you look, there's no one there."

I walked around the hotel area alone one time, just to see if the ghostly girl would make her presence known. She didn't, but standing there in the hallway looking at the row of rooms, I felt a chill run through my body. It was probably just the thought of standing in the exact same place as those gunfighters and cowhands did in the days of Hell's Half Acre. I walked around the corner and back toward the staircase, as so many men had done in the past, and stopped in room 11 to make a few notes. There was no scent of perfume or soft touches by unseen hands, and as I wrote, I hoped that the girl had found some relief for her grieving heart, at least for a little while.

Barber's Books 817.335.5469
Greene's Antiques 817.820.0196
215 W. 8th St.
Fort Worth, TX 76102

# The Gentleman Resident of Del Frisco's Steakhouse

Del Frisco's Double Eagle Steak House in downtown Fort Worth has a national reputation for serving up one of the best steaks you'll ever plunge a fork into. Don't take my word for it; just try their ten-ounce Carpetbagger Ribeye, and you will know why.

I've got to tell you, chasing ghost stories in restaurants is a dangerous thing for me. I'll be looking for someone to talk to about the spirits in the place, when all of a sudden I'll get a whiff of some epicurean delight, and I'm suddenly discussing grilling techniques with the chef.

While I didn't completely lose focus on my mission to their restaurant, I did learn that a Del Frisco's steak is cooked in a broiler at about 1,800 degrees. You're going to have to pardon my little detour here, but I was so taken by my steak that I had to do a little digging on how they produce their award-winning dishes. Anyway, cooking it as they do sears the meat on both sides so that

absolutely no juices escape. I've just got to figure out how to do this at home.

One last note, and then we'll move on to the ghost there. Believe me, while working on this chapter, I wondered at exactly what point I'd switched gears from ghost stories to restaurant reviews, but what the heck. I just have to pass on one more cooking tip for all of you who ever put a match to a pile of charcoal out on the back patio: The grade of meat you're using matters a lot more than you think. When I asked what they used at Del Frisco's to get their steaks to taste so wonderful, I was told that the grade of beef served there was USDA Prime, the highest grade available. In fact, the prime grade represents only two percent of all the beef in the country each year. When I asked where I could purchase such a high grade for my grill at home, I got a disappointing answer. You see, it is a product so rare that it is generally not available to the average consumer. Sure, I was a little bummed out, but I did make a mental note to start shopping for higher grade beef when I cooked out. Meanwhile, I just dug back into my steak. I have to say, that is one of the things I love the most about looking for restaurant ghosts—there's always an excuse to sit down for a meal!

I didn't leave hungry from Del Frisco's. Between the heaping portion of chunky mashed potatoes and the huge salad, along with the steak itself, I needed a while to just sit and enjoy the meal. It was the perfect time to ask a few questions about ghosts—and to spare you from any more of my culinary wanderings.

Like several other places in this book, Del Frisco's Double Eagle Steak House is located in the "Hell's Half Acre" part of Fort Worth, which was a stop on the Kansas cattle trail back in the 1870s. Hell's Half Acre was located on the southern end of the city and was a collection of saloons, bawdy houses, and gambling dens. It definitely wasn't the place for anyone from polite society to visit. Daily activities included drinking, gambling, brawling, cockfighting, and of course, visiting the ladies of ill-repute at their houses there in the Acre.

By 1881 the area had spread to over two-and-a-half acres, according to the *Fort Worth Democrat* newspaper. Despite the concern expressed by the good citizens of Fort Worth, the area continued to boom in order to serve the trail hands and railroad workers who drifted through town. Eventually, it covered the blocks from Seventh Street down to Fifteenth Street around 1900. When Fort Worth was partitioned into three political wards, the area assumed the new moniker of "The Bloody Third Ward."

Outlaws such as Butch Cassidy and the Sundance Kid (for which Fort Worth's Sundance Square is named), the Sam Bass Gang, Timothy ("Longhair Jim") Courtright, Luke Short, Bat Masterson, Wyatt Earp, Doc Holliday, and many others reportedly used the section of town as an oasis of sorts while passing through Fort Worth, blending in with the likes of prostitutes, conmen, gunmen, card sharps, and all the other ilk that the Acre attracted.

During that time period, the building that is now Del Frisco's Double Eagle Steak House was actually a bathhouse. The legend goes that a gentleman had stopped in for a bath after a night of drinking, gambling, and carousing. He must have angered one of the shadier characters in the Acre, because as he enjoyed his hot bath that had been hand-filled for him by a lovely young lady, an unseen gunman shot him in the back of the head. He died right there in the tub. Whether it was the sudden death of the patron or some unfinished business there in the Acre, the spirit of the man has reportedly stayed with the building throughout the years.

That's the story as I heard it, anyway. No matter what might have happened in the building back in its rougher days, there seems to be a mysterious presence in the building today. The staff has reported inexplicable footsteps in the restaurant after business hours, when the front doors were locked and the place was being closed for the evening. Other occurrences attributed to the spirit that visits Del Frisco's are small areas of extremely frigid air that one will happen upon suddenly, gentle touches on the shoulder even though there isn't another person near, and a general feeling of just being watched in an empty room. The activity reportedly takes place all over the restaurant, from the upstairs bar to the downstairs banquet room, as the specter moves slowly through the building.

I didn't have any supernatural experiences on my visit, but given the extraordinary meal, I'm going to be doing a little investigation there every chance I get!

Del Frisco's Double Eagle Steak House
812 Main St.
Fort Worth, TX 76102
817.877.3999

# The Cowboy Spirit of the Stockyards Hotel

Since I enjoy history so much, I immediately fell in love with the three-story hotel on Exchange Street in Fort Worth. Bonnie and Clyde stayed here. So have Willie Nelson, George Strait, Garth Brooks, and Gary P. Nunn. Some of the most powerful cattle barons in the days of the Old West have spent the night in Fort Worth's Stockyards Hotel, right down the hall from the most common of cowboys. One lonely gunfighter also boarded there, and after being shot down in the street in front of the hotel, he seems reluctant to leave. It is a very fitting place for him to reside, though; the Stockyards Hotel traces its history back to the very birth of Fort Worth.

In the early to mid-1800s, Fort Worth was a town struggling to survive. It was an army outpost, protecting settlers from Indian attacks, and there were very few businesses lining the streets. That all turned around when the cattle drives began to stop in town on their journeys northward along the Chisholm Trail. As the century came to an end, the town had exploded with saloons, blacksmith shops, gambling halls, bordellos, and livestock yards— just like the Hell's Half Acre area—everything the gentleman traveler or lonesome cowboy might desire.

In 1907 Colonel William Thannisch erected a building at the corner of Exchange and Main Streets that, among other things, housed the Stock Yards Club where visitors to the city could get a room for the evening, complete with the luxury of an indoor bathroom on every single floor. From foreign dignitaries to the lowliest cowhands, everyone came to know about the famous hotel in the stockyards.

The Stockyards Hotel has certainly gathered its share of stories over the years. The notorious outlaws Bonnie and Clyde spent a night in room 305 back in 1933. There are several different tales about their visit; one account suggests they were hiding out from authorities that were chasing them across Texas after one of their legendary bank robberies. Another version has the bandits casing a nearby bank from their hotel room window, plotting to rob it in an attempt that was later foiled, although I had a waitress in Booger Red's Saloon tell me, "There was a bank right across the street, and Bonnie and Clyde hit it the morning after they stayed at the hotel."

Over the years the name changed to the Chandler Hotel, then the Plaza Hotel, and finally the Stockyards Hotel. Throughout all of the name changes and the other history of the property, a perpetual resident continued to make himself known.

The story of the spirit reportedly dates back to 1910, when a cowboy who was passing through town booked a room for the evening. After a night in the rowdy stockyards, a gunfight ensued out in front of the hotel, and the fellow was shot and killed. For some reason, though, he decided to hang around the hotel, and his presence has been felt ever since. The hotel staff named him Jesse, a moniker by which he is referred to this day.

Jesse has been occasionally spotted roaming the hallways of the second and third floors. He seems to be a gentle soul, harmlessly wandering through the hotel, never stopping to interact with any of the guests. Jesse has also been seen on the landing of the staircase that leads from the lobby up to the second floor. The Marine Creek Terrace, an indoor/outdoor banquet area that overlooks the historic Stockyards District's Marine Creek, is a place frequented by Jesse. It is not only the ghostly form of Jesse that indicates his presence, however. When the night is still and the hotel is very quiet, the sound of footsteps can be heard in the hallways, accompanied by the jingle of cowboy spurs.

The staircase landing where Jesse has been known to frequent

Mr. Lonnie Allen, the director of sales for the Stockyards Hotel, told me of another spirit that inhabits the property. "We do have a story about 'Jake,' a long-time employee here. Jake was a houseman that would go and knock on the door to a room [to deliver a message] and sounded like Lurch from the Addams Family. Needless to say, a lot of people would freak out. Nonetheless, Jake passed away after twenty years of service." According to Mr. Allen, Jake may still be reporting for duty at the hotel. Many odd occurrences are attributed to him. "Rumor has it that all sorts of strange things happen at night. For instance, the elevator will start going up and down the floors all by itself. Also, mysterious calls will come into the front desk from an unknown extension. You cannot put the call on hold or transfer the call."

One of the hallways where ghostly footsteps are sometimes heard

I enjoyed my visit to the hotel and gave both Jake and Jesse a chance to get to know me. The hallways were quiet, and I listened intently for any footsteps other than my own, specifically ones with the tell-tale jingle of spurs. I paused on the landing of the staircase, hoping to catch a glimpse of Jesse, and then took a seat on one of the leather couches in the lobby. Many people passed by, but they all seemed to be from the earthly plane, and not one of the hotel's ghostly residents. After a while, I resolved myself to the fact that the spirits weren't out and about that day.

There was something else there, however: the spirit of the historical old hotel itself. Had Clyde Barrow sat on the exact same location on the couch, speaking to Bonnie in hushed tones about the bank across the street? And what about the legions of cowboys from the Chisholm Trail days, whose footsteps I may have been unknowingly tracing as I wandered the hotel. Could they have come and gone without leaving some trace of themselves there? It gave me pause to contemplate all the sights that the hotel must have seen, and left me with a sense of awe. I took one last look in the huge lobby mirror, ran a comb through my hair, and wondered what cattle baron might have done the same thing many decades ago. The Stockyards Hotel is truly a magnificent place, full of history and wonder, not to mention a few ghosts that just might make your stay even more interesting!

The Stockyards Hotel
109 E. Exchange Ave.
Fort Worth, TX 76106
Phone: 800.423.8471
Web: http://www.stockyardshotel.com

# The Spirits of the Cattle Baron's Mansion

Standing majestically in the Quality Hill area of Fort Worth is a mansion known as "Thistle Hill." It has a rich history, steeped in the bygone era of the majestic cattle barons. It is certainly a place that might have a spirit or two, but when I made some initial inquiries about any supernatural activity there, I was told that Thistle Hill is not haunted. Not no way, not no how. It's just a beautiful old building that has been restored to its turn-of-the-century elegance. Upon hearing this, I heaved a disappointed sigh, then flipped my #2 pencil around and started erasing it from my ghost-hunters notebook.

A very interesting thing happened several weeks later, as I sat at a library table buried in stacks of newspaper microfilm boxes. I found an interesting article about Thistle Hill. It seems that several years ago the restored three-story Georgian Revival house was opened up to a paranormal investigation group, and the events

were chronicled in the article that was in front of me. It took a while to locate one of the investigators, but I finally hooked up with Andy Grieser, who was part of that ghost-hunting evening spent at Thistle Hill.

It seems like the perfect place to spend a night looking for spirits. The house was built in 1904 by William T. Waggoner, one of the legendary Fort Worth cattle barons, as a gift to his daughter and son-in-law. Electra Waggoner had fallen in love with and married Mr. A. B. Wharton Jr. of Philadelphia, and her father was afraid she would move to Pennsylvania with her new husband. To entice them to stay, Waggoner engaged Fort Worth's best-known architectural firm, Sanguinet and Staats, to produce a stunning home in one of the most prestigious neighborhoods in town. The result was Thistle Hill, built for the enormous, unthinkable sum of $38,000. The newlyweds moved in and became an integral part of Fort Worth society. There aren't any reportings of ghostly activity in the house at that time, but then, the history of Thistle Hill was just getting started.

Electra's father divided his fortune among his three children, and she received a large share including land and livestock.

Deciding to move out of the city, she and her husband put the house up for sale in 1910 and moved out to their ranch.

Thistle Hill was purchased by Winfield Scott, a real estate tycoon. He reportedly paid $90,000 for the property, then immediately launched a renovation effort that would cost an additional $100,000. Unfortunately, Scott died before it was complete, leaving his widow, Elizabeth, to live in the house and finish raising their son alone. The tale becomes even more tragic, however. After her death in 1938, her son ran through his inheritance in very short order and was forced to put Thistle Hill up for sale.

The mansion was purchased in 1940 by the Girls Service League of Fort Worth for the miniscule sum of $17,500. The organization was dedicated to the assistance of underprivileged young women, housing them and helping the girls to get on their feet. Some people were disappointed that the stately home was being used as a women's boardinghouse, but as many mansions were being destroyed in the name of progress, the League's presence actually saved the house from demolition. The ladies occupied the house until 1968, at which time they put Thistle Hill up for sale and let it stand empty.

A historic preservation organization named "Save the Scott House" was formed by citizens who did not want the house to be demolished, and by 1976 they had raised the money to purchase the home; it sold for $375,000. Restoration began on the house, with meticulous attention to detail, and today the home is maintained by the nonprofit organization renamed Texas Heritage, Inc., and is open to the public for tours and special events. One such event, that will likely not be repeated, was to let a paranormal investigation group spend the night in the old house.

Andy Grieser reports, "Our team of ghost hunters first visited Thistle Hill in 1989. At one point, we heard horrible noises, like chains being dragged. We finally cornered the source: an ice machine. But weird stuff did happen. An envelope of newspaper clippings and a flashlight left on a downstairs table disappeared, only to turn up later in the billiards room."

There's no lack of restless souls at the mansion, according to Grieser. "A woman in white periodically appears on the grand staircase, and a man sporting a handlebar mustache and tennis togs sometimes looks down from the top of the stairs. Work crews regularly quit during renovations in the late 1980s after hearing mysterious music from the sealed-off third-floor ballroom."

The focus of the supernatural activity during Mr. Grieser's stay in the house seemed to be a 97-year-old rocking chair. When they had arrived for their evening of ghost hunting, the chair and other pieces of furniture in what was once Thistle Hill's grand ball-room were draped in heavy, protective plastic sheets. In the course of the evening, Mr. Grieser's group explored the house. When they had traversed each of the floors very thoroughly, they returned to the ballroom where a surprise awaited them. The shrouded rocker they had left only moments before now sat on the ballroom floor completely uncovered and facing away from the door.

After standing there in shock for a few moments, one of the team members covered it back up, and as the plastic was draped back over the chair, Grieser remembers, "its crackle was too loud to be missed in the dead of night. How had the chair's unveiling gone unnoticed?"

When the group got back down to the ground floor, one of the members explained, "That chair was covered when the tour got to the ballroom, I know it. I covered it again before we came down." The group went back upstairs, and while the chair was still covered, it had been turned away from the door again, as Mr. Grieser says, "as if to watch dancers who hadn't graced the ballroom in almost a century."

At 12:45 A.M., there was another incident with the chair. One of the team members looked back at it, and once again, the plastic sheet had been removed, as if some unseen presence was insistent on sitting there. Grieser had no explanation. "A group of ghost hunters standing mere feet away saw and heard nothing."

As the early morning hours passed, the group made another pass around the house, and Mr. Grieser had the chance to enjoy the beauty and history of Thistle Hill. "At 5 A.M. we are walking around the ballroom, disappointed by the still-covered chairs. Squinting into the dark, I imagined the parties held in this room, with an orchestra playing on the veranda while the city's elite swept to and fro in elegant garb. I could almost see it, two or three couples in white gliding across the wooden floor." A beautiful mental picture of a scene that probably often took place at the house. As the group stood there in the silence and darkness of the ballroom, Mr. Grieser recalls, "Somewhere, a rocking chair creaked."

Thistle Hill
1509 Pennsylvania Ave.
Fort Worth, TX 76104
Phone: 817.336.1212
Web: http://www.thistlehill.org

# The Lilac Ghost of Log Cabin Village

When you walk under the rustic archway that proclaims "Log Cabin Village," you step directly into the eighteen hundreds. Nestled among the trees in this world of the past, you'll find yourself standing in the middle of a collection of seven log cabins that have been transported here from Parker, Tarrant, and Milam Counties, all dating from the 1840s to 1860. In a world where movie sets and amusement parks replicate such structures every day, it's easy to shrug your shoulders and just start walking along the path. The important thing to remember, though, is that these houses are the genuine articles. They were built by the families who lived in them, and the structures only narrowly escaped destruction. Maybe that explains some of the unusual activity that has been noticed in one of the cabins.

Log Cabin Park had a rocky beginning. Back in the 1950s, a man named Fred Cotton was a devotee of Texas history and a president of the Texas State Historical Association. He took a good look around and realized that the log cabins of the past were quickly being replaced with cookie-cutter houses of the modern world. Mr. Cotton made it his business to start a push for

preservation of log cabin life, and he was joined in his efforts by W.A. Schmid Jr. The Pioneer Texas Heritage Committee was formed, and the city of Fort Worth was approached to aid in the project.

The committee found six log houses, all from the 1800s and each an example of a different type of construction. While the log houses were being identified and cataloged, the Parks Department of Fort Worth was searching for a location that would serve as a home to the cabins. A spot near the Trinity River in Forest Park turned out to be the most desirable place, but once the six cabins were moved there, things began to get a little rough. Money became tight for the project, to the point where restoration of the houses was completely out of the question, and furnishing them with period pieces was only a far-away dream.

The Heritage Committee was determined, though, and launched a myriad of fund-raising activities. The people of Fort Worth responded in grand fashion, and it soon appeared that the tough times were starting to pass. By 1963 the cabins had been preserved and restored, and two years later responsibility for the site was transferred to the Fort Worth Parks and Recreation

Department. In April of 1966, Log Cabin Village officially opened to the public, and the dreams of Mr. Cotton and Mr. Schmid were realized.

The village served as a "living history" museum, where visitors could see the log homes of the pioneer days and observe artisans spinning thread, grinding corn, making wax candles, blacksmithing, and other activities of the period. It became a popular place for both tourists to the city and school field trips.

In 1975 another cabin was added to the park, and with it came something other than the history. The home had belonged to a man named Foster who lived in the cabin with his young son back in the 1850s, along with Miss Jane Holt, a nanny for the boy. It is in the Foster cabin that many encounters with a gentle spirit have occurred.

Because of its haunted reputation, the two-story log cabin that had belonged to the Fosters was my first stop in the park. It wasn't hard to find; since it is one of the larger structures, it serves as the Visitor's Center and General Store where guests can pick up a memento of their visit. I managed to corral one of the friendly ladies who work there, and I asked about the cabin's history.

"This was the last one added to the park," she said and went on to reiterate the story of the Fosters. "No one knows for sure, but speculation is that Mr. Foster and Miss Holt fell in love and married. We don't have a record of exactly when it happened, but I hear that the couple appears on a census roll together, along with the boy." Of course, I had to ask about the ghost.

I can always tell when someone has encountered a spirit at a location that I'm visiting, because they get a sly smile on their face that seems to say, "Ah, you know my little secret." This lady was no different, even laughing a little before telling me the story. "Well, it would seem that Jane probably died in the cabin. Ten years after she's found on the census roll, she just disappears. The next census shows only Mr. Foster and his son. Any number of illnesses could have taken her life back then, medicine being what it was at the time. There were two bedrooms upstairs, and we think she passed on in the one belonging to her and Mr. Foster. That's where some people have claimed to see something."

The Foster cabin

She went on to explain that the upstairs bedrooms had initially been open for the public to tour, but after a few minor accidents on the stairs, it had to be closed for insurance reasons. The upstairs area basically consists of two bedrooms separated by a staircase, which is all now used for storage by the park. "Most of the experiences are simply the scent of flowers, that I'm told are lilac blooms," the lady told me. "You'll walk right into it, just like it was a cloud of perfume. That's how you know that Jane is around. That happens both upstairs and down here in the gift shop. The people who have seen her, though, tell me that she appears as kind of a misty figure caught out of the corner of their eye. She's wearing a dark skirt with a light blouse but fades away before anyone can get a good look at her."

I asked if she'd seen Jane, and the lady just smiled. "No, I haven't actually seen her. I've found the scent of flowers, though. When it happens, you can just stand there and feel that someone's near you. It's very peaceful, really, and a wonderful experience."

Other visitors were starting to drift in, so I said my thank-you and let the lady move on. I wanted to explore the rest of the village, but before leaving I stood quietly in the Foster cabin and just soaked in the ambiance. Maybe it was the perfume of the lady I'd been talking to, but before I left, I could swear that I detected the sweet smell of flowers in the air.

Log Cabin Village
2100 Log Cabin Village Lane
Fort Worth, TX 76109
Phone: 817.926.5881
Web: http://www.logcabinvillage.org

# The Grandfatherly Blessings of Peters Brothers Hats

Let me say up front, Peters Brothers Hats is not haunted; in fact, they're kind of sensitive to the word and really don't like to hear their place described as such. But while there is no ghostly presence that lingers in the store, Joe Peters Sr. is pretty sure his grandfather keeps an eye on them, just to insure that things are going well.

When I contacted Mr. Peters and told him about this book, I asked if I could include a story about his grandfather and how he likes to look in on them from time to time. He told me, "I think my grandfather would like that!"

You see, Joe Peters' grandfather was an interesting fellow. Tom Peters started the family business back in 1911 with his brother, Jim. They were Greek immigrants who first got their start in the shoeshine business down in Waco. But they soon moved up to a small shop in the rough and rugged part of Fort Worth known as "Hell's Half Acre," a section that gained notoriety with the cattle drives that came though town, as you've read about in other parts of this book.

Their shine business flourished, and since Tom had worked in a hat factory back in Greece, he had enough knowledge of the trade to add a hat refurbishing side to their business.

While Jim minded the store back home, Tom went to Pennsylvania and worked for John Stetson for a while, where he honed his skills. Then he came back and started making hats under the Peters Brothers brand in Fort Worth.

The story of Peters Brothers Hats is an important part of the city's history, because the business' growth mirrored that of Fort Worth. In the waning days of Hell's Half Acre, the shine and hat business accommodated the ruffian and gentlemen trade alike. As the notorious side of town faded away and commerce began to take root in the downtown area, the shop became a location for the discriminating man to find just the perfect hat.

Jim passed away in the early thirties, leaving Tom to run the business, and he used his brother's insurance money to purchase a building two doors down. Like Joe Peters Sr. likes to say today, "we're at our *new location*, where we've only been since 1933."

Tom Peters purchased the building for fifteen thousand dollars, totally refurbished it, and set up a complete men's store. A gentleman could purchase a new hat or have his old one blocked, get his shoes shined, and even have his suit pressed while he waited.

During World War II, Tom set up a military hat factory upstairs, which supplied the nation's servicemen all the way through the Korean War. During the World War, the shoeshine business was particularly big at the store, since the soldiers from Fort Bowie would bring their business to town to get their shoes and boots shined. Joe Sr. describes it perfectly: "Back then, there was a piano in the place, and one of the shine men would play ragtime. The rest of the guys would snap their shine rags in time to the music, so it was kind of like a shoeshine and a show altogether. My grandfather always liked this section of Fort Worth, because it was in the smack-dab middle of town, right between the railroad station and the courthouse. A trolley car went out from 9th Street to the west side of town, so that traffic came into the store as well."

Joe started working for his grandfather in 1972. He came in to work in the hat shop full time in 1986 and then slowly took more responsibility in the business. Tom Peters was not one to give up working as he got older, though. He wasn't into fishing, hunting, or playing golf; he wanted to just work in the store and learn new things. In fact, the old fellow always said, "A day that you don't learn something new is just a wasted day." I like that. One of my own favorite quotes is by Michelangelo, at 87 years of age: "*Ancoro imparo*," which means, "I am still learning."

Tom Peters sounds like a wonderful fellow, but no one can describe him like his grandson Joe Sr.: "He would give hats to special people. And when he sold a hat, he'd teach the man how to put it on, telling him that 'if you do it right, you'll get a prize.' He'd show them how to do it, including the Texas Touch along the brim of the hat. He would then give them a silver dollar. I've had old men come in and show me a silver dollar and tell me that my grandfather gave it to them when they bought a hat many years ago."

It is wonderful to watch Joe Sr. talk about him. There's a smile on his face that just can't be described. "My grandfather loved gadgets; he had an electric garage door opener in 1949, an electric

One of the many hat displays at Peters Brothers

water cooler with a five gallon bottle in his house in 1949, and a color TV as soon as it came out. One of the things that he'd love today is the World Wide Web and the fact that Peters Brothers Hats has a web site up!"

As tough as it may have been for him, Tom Peters eventually had to slow down. He worked until he was 98½ years old, always reminding his patrons to never forget their hat. One day he was sitting in a chair in the store when the leg broke, and he fell back against a hat display case. He hit his neck, and the blow affected his left hand. He could still use it, just not as effectively. Tom didn't work much after that, although that determined old man lived to see almost 101 years. He passed away in 1991, and missed 101 by six weeks.

Joe Sr. says, "I guess I'm the old man, now." Maybe, since his son Joe Jr. is very active in the store. When I visited, he wasn't sitting behind a desk or running the front register; he was in the work area, carefully crafting a hat. I got a chance to look around the shop and was amazed at their selections and the personal attention

I saw them giving the customers. I wear a Resistol felt and a Stetson straw, both of which were purchased at some nondescript store that I can't remember. However, my next hat will come from Peters Brothers Hats; it is one of those special places you just don't find anymore.

The main part of the store

Although Tom Peters has passed on to much greater things than this world has to offer, he may take the occasional opportunity to check back in on the business. According to Joe Sr., "We feel the spirit of my grandfather here in the store. Sometimes a hat will just fall off of a rack on its own or off of a wall hook, or a broom that's leaning against a wall will fall over by itself, and we'll say 'well, that's Granddad.' It seems that if we're just goofing off and not really working, that broom will fall and they'll be a loud crash. Or if we've made a big sale, that will happen, and I've had a feeling that he's either approving or disapproving at the time. You feel proud, like he knows what's going on."

I can only imagine. My own grandfather was a Southern Baptist minister in East Texas who could pull more bass out of a lake than anyone else in the state, and I spent my adolescent life growing up next door to him. What I wouldn't give to know that he looks in from time to time, just to see how things are going. That would be wonderful beyond words. Joe Peters Sr., I have to say, you really are blessed.

Peters Brothers Hats
909 Houston Street
Fort Worth, TX 76102
Toll Free: 1.800.TXS.HATS (800.897.4287)
Web: http://www.petersbros.com

# Freaky Happenings at the Jett Building

I'd heard that a parade of businesses had occupied the Jett Building in the Sundance Square area of downtown Fort Worth, so when I finally found myself in front of 400 Main Street I was delighted to see there was a Jamba Juice located there!

The afternoon was getting warm, so I stepped right up to the counter and ordered a Banana Berry, my favorite mixture off of their smoothie menu!

While it was being made, I walked around the shop just to see if I noticed anything out of the ordinary, but it seemed like any juice bar in America today. That's okay, though, because I knew I was only there to take a cursory look around. The real story would come later, when I hooked up with someone who'd actually owned a business in the old Jett Building.

For the time being, though, I just accepted my custom-made smoothie from the gentleman behind the counter and took a walk around the building.

An incredible mural of a cattle drive is painted on the southern side of the building, and I found out that it is named "The Chisholm Trail." For those readers who are more familiar with the arts than I

The Chisholm Trail mural on the Jett Building

am, I also found out that the artwork is a trompe l'oeil mural painted by the artist Richard Haas. Haas has painted dozens of architectural murals throughout the world since the early 1970s. This one was created to commemorate the Fort Worth segment of the Chisholm Trail cattle drives of 1867-1875.

The building itself was supposedly completed in 1907, and I was told that it appears to be modeled after Frank Lloyd Wright's Larkin Building in Buffalo, New York. When it was opened, the three-story brick structure was originally the home of the Northern Texas Traction Co., which operated the Interurban Railway with service to Dallas and Cleburne.

An impressive place, no doubt about it. The most interesting aspects of the Jett Building came to light, however, when I had the opportunity to speak to Sheila Walker, who was once a merchant there. The first thing out of her mouth was, "Some freaky things happen in that place."

Ms. Walker purchased Fort Worth Books and Video, which was located there prior to 1988. In her own words, she bought it

The Jamba Juice frontage of the Jett Building

"lock, stock, and barrel." Starting with that seed of growth, she opened "The Book Cellar" in the basement and first floor, an enterprise that was open for business between 1988 and 1990.

When she had the bookstore, the second and third floors were vacant and had been for some time. They had once been used as building offices. Unfortunately, the air conditioning never seemed to work on both floors simultaneously, even though they were both on the same unit. The electricity was also constantly misbehaving, to the point where the floors were basically unusable.

One of the most interesting features in the store was a ten-foot-wide beautiful staircase that went from the basement to the first floor. The way the store was laid out, the checkout counter was located at the top of the stairs.

One evening after they had closed for the day, Ms. Walker was standing at the counter with the store manager, when she glanced down the stairs and saw a man standing there at the bottom. She looked away, then back downstairs to see that he was suddenly gone. Thinking someone was still in the store, she went down and circled the lower floor of the bookstore. There wasn't a single person there; the floor was deserted. Ms. Walker climbed back upstairs and continued closing out the register, without thinking anything else about the incident. The manager who was with her suddenly looked down the stairs, then hurried down them. In a few minutes she was coming back up, and Ms. Walker asked what she was doing. The manager told her the exact same story as her own. They both looked back down at the same time, and the man was standing there once again. Ms. Walker remembers that he was very pale, with a black suit, black cowboy boots, and black hair, with every item appearing to be 1800s period attire. When they looked back at each other and then back down, the man had mysteriously disappeared once again.

Ms. Walker told me that incident was the only time she actually saw a figure, but odd things seemed to be happening all the time. At night in the basement, for instance, there was some mischief occurring with the books. The display shelves were A-frame, so the books themselves were leaning in and it would be virtually impossible for them to fall off of the shelves on their own. Nevertheless, many mornings when the staff opened up the store, there were books lying on the floor in the aisles downstairs. Although everyone thought it was odd, they just got used to living with it.

The books on the floor were never harmed, which is also very strange, since a fall from up on a shelf could damage the spine or corners of the book; yet these were always in pristine condition. Ms. Walker told me that for a while they looked for a pattern to see if the ghosts happened to be interested in one particular genre of literature or another, but there was no indication other than some spirit just being a little mischievous.

At one point The Book Cellar was going to add a coffee bar in the basement so that the patrons could sip a latte or mocha while browsing the shelves. Ms. Walker and a friend were working on it very late at night so as not to interfere with the day's business, and in fact the job went into the wee morning hours. As they were working, her friend jumped up a couple of times and ran upstairs. Each time she just came back down and returned to their work. Ms. Walker finally asked what was going on, and her friend

**132**

*The Ghosts of Fort Worth*

explained that she'd heard footsteps upstairs, and she was searching for whomever might be walking around up there. Of course, she'd never found anyone; they were in the building alone.

Ms. Walker had heard the footsteps many times before, however, so she wasn't surprised by the story. Each time they "walked" from a back corner of the room toward the front door and sounded like a woman in heels stepping across a wooden floor. The footsteps never retraced themselves, never moved in a circle, and never seemed to vary from their set direction.

Noises were another manifestation of the spirits that inhabited the Jett Building. Although she never heard actual voices herself, Ms. Walker told me that several of the people on staff had shared stories with her about hearing talking in the aisles of the bookstore while they were closing up, even though the building was empty and the front door was locked.

The security guards in the building were even witness to one of the incidents involving a noise or two. As Ms. Walker explained it, the way the bookstore worked at the end of the day was that an employee would close up the register on the basement floor, and then that person would come up to the first floor to help close out the register at the counter at the top of the stairs. One evening during that process, while two workers were at the first floor register, party-like noise was heard on the second floor. There were feet shuffling just like there was a full-fledged dance party up on the second floor. The workers were afraid that some people had broken into the upper floors and were reveling in the empty space, so they immediately called building security. The guards arrived and went directly upstairs to check things out. They found absolutely nothing—just empty, dark floors. The guards came back downstairs to tell the workers that everything was fine, and just as they were in the middle of saying there was nothing upstairs, a loud clumping and thumping started up there once again. The guards looked at each other, then at the workers, and said, "Pack up, let's go home!"

Ms. Walker was kind enough to tell me one more story about the place, but this one was concerning a former owner, who had been very skeptical about the building actually being haunted.

There is a room downstairs that had, in the past, been used as an office because it was not finished out for the public. It contains the heat and air conditioner controls and other industrial aspects of running the building. The door is a large, wooden monstrosity, very heavy, and is hard to open or close because it drags on the concrete floor either way. The light switch for the room is about four feet inside, so when you go in you are in the dark for a couple of steps.

One evening, after making sure he was alone in the building and locking the main doors, the former owner had gone inside the room, when the lights suddenly switched off and the door slammed shut. Something had not only closed the door, but locked it from the outside. He was stuck there until the morning, and when he was let out the next day, the man was as white as a sheet. The fellow left the building, not to return for several days.

After her story, I wondered if the former owner had ever spoken about the ghosts. I was delighted to discover an article in an October 31, 1986 edition of *The Dallas Morning News* entitled, "Chance of a Ghost: Strange occurrences at Fort Worth business keep workers on edge" by Dan Malone. Not only did the owner of Fort Worth Books and Video describe the previous story told to me by Ms. Walker, but also had many other comments about the building. The most telling was a simple "There are things that go bump in the night. It's a puzzlement."

The same kinds of footsteps that Ms. Walker described have apparently been heard there for years. "Employees working in the basement reported hearing steps pacing from a first-floor vault to an old elevator shaft. But the steps were heard when no one was upstairs, and they followed a path that would have required a person to walk through shelves filled with books," the previous owner said.

One day he heard the steps for himself. They walked right up behind him, and he felt a tap on the shoulder. Turning quickly around, he saw that he was alone in the room.

Something else caught my eye in the article, though. In my research, I'd found that the building was completed in 1907. *The Dallas Morning News* stated that tax records show it was built in

1920, and the former owner reported seeing an old photograph of Main Street that indicates the building may have been there since the late 1800s.

According to the article, "City directories show the building served as a train depot during the 1920s and 1930s, was vacant in 1940, housed a sandwich shop from 1950 through 1960, and was home to a blueprint company in 1970. It was vacant again in the mid-1970s and was used by Bass architects and construction workers in the early 1980s. Former Tarrant County sheriff Lon Evans recalls a pool hall in the building at one point."

Perhaps the origins of the building are as big a mystery as the things that go on there.

The inside of the Jett Building is now Jamba Juice

Although Ms. Walker saw the ghostly man and experienced other harmless phenomenon, she was never really frightened of the phantoms that were there. Perhaps she got along with the ghosts in the Jett Building a little better than most folks. She found them to mainly be pranksters, who were having a little harmless fun. If they were taking the books off the shelves at night when she had her store there, I can only wonder what they do with the Jamba Juice machines when everyone has gone home. Maybe the man in the dark suit, like me, is a Banana Berry person.

The Jett Building
(now Jamba Juice)
400 Main Street
Fort Worth, TX 76102

# The Spectral Ladies of Miss Molly's

I would have missed a wonderful location to feature in this book, had it not been for Vicki Isaacs from Metroplex Paranormal Investigations. We were covering another location their ghost-hunting group had visited, when Vicki happened to mention Miss Molly's Bed and Breakfast in the historic old Fort Worth Stockyards.

Now, as you may be able to tell from other chapters in this book, I love the Stockyards. They're full of rich history and color, and I can't visit there without wanting to don my cowboy hat, pull on my lizard skin boots, and take time out for a two-step at one of its saloons.

Miss Molly's was a place I hadn't had the pleasure of visiting before this book, though, so hearing about it was a real treat. Like several other locations I'd found, the original building started out as a place for the lovely "tainted angels" of the rougher side of Fort Worth to entertain the cowhands and travelers that passed through town.

In today's world of the Stockyards, however, the building is host not only to the bed and breakfast upstairs, but also to the Star Café downstairs—one of the highly acclaimed restaurants in the area.

So what ghosts reside in Miss Molly's? Well, apparently they are figures from the hotel's past. It was built in 1910 when the cattle business in Fort Worth was booming, and it was used as a boardinghouse for those having business in the Stockyards: cattlemen, businessmen, traveling salesmen, and even the average cowboy who'd won enough money in a game of chance to afford the luxury of a room for the evening.

The boardinghouse rented out rooms by the night, week, or longer for those having extended business in the yards. By the 1920s it was still a respectable place for gentlemen to stay and was operated by a proper hostess named Amelia Eimer. The name of the establishment at the time was "The Palace Rooms," and the way Ms. Eimer ran the place, it probably was a palace for its time, although the construction was very simple: a central parlor surrounded by nine rooms.

In time "The Palace Rooms" became the "The Oasis," playing to the same clientele. It wasn't until a decade or so later that the real moneymaking potential of the property became evident. Two of the nation's major meat packing companies, the Armour company and the Swift company, had set up shop in the Stockyards and were attracting plant employees, railroad workers, and other visitors to the area.

In the 1940s Miss Josie King seized the opportunity to use the building to capitalize on the hoards of men passing through town. Miss King converted the boardinghouse into a bawdy house named the Gayette Hotel, where the house girls were paraded out into the center parlor for gentlemen to make their selection.

As the cattle trade began to fade in Fort Worth, so did Miss King's business. The Gayette Hotel was eventually closed, and the building was vacant until it was purchased for use as an art gallery—quite a cultural change from its former trade! It worked out well, though, because individual artists were allowed to purchase space in one of the old hotel rooms in which to work and display their wares. It operated smoothly and quietly so very little is known about these days, especially in regard to any paranormal activity in the building.

In 1989, however, Mark and Susan Hancock purchased the old hotel. It was completely restored and refurbished then given the name "Miss Molly's" after the lead cow on a cattle drive, who drovers usually referred to as the "Molly." Speaking of which, while you're in the Stockyards don't miss the live cattle drive that happens twice daily, at 11:30 A.M. and 4:00 P.M., weather permitting of course. The cowboys take the herd from the Fort Worth Livestock Exchange Building at 131 E. Exchange Avenue, down Exchange, and then back to their holding pens behind the Exchange Building. It's a slice of the Old West and Stockyards history that is definitely worth seeing.

The Hancocks furnished each of eight rooms in the upper floor hotel in antiques from the heyday period of the Fort Worth Stockyards and gave each room a name with an associated theme. For example, when you visit you can choose from Miss Josie's room, named after Miss Josie King, the madam during the 1940s; Miss Amelia's, from Amelia Eimer, the prim and proper proprietress of the 1920s; the Cowboy room that is reminiscent of a bunkhouse; and others including the Cattlemen's, the Rodeo, the Gunslinger, the Oilman, and the Railroader, each of which has its own décor and amenities.

If you stick your head into each of the rooms at Miss Molly's while you're there, you'll find adornments from lace curtains to

The Exchange Street entrance used by many a trail-hand

cast-iron beds, antique quilts, and exquisite old furniture. One of the highlights of the visit is being served breakfast in the central parlor, beneath a beautiful stained glass skylight, in the exact same location where gentlemen clients used to select their lady for an evening's entertainment.

Compared to the boardinghouse resident of days gone by, travelers today are well pampered. Guests are greeted every day with coffee, tea, and juice, fresh fruit, and hearty specialty breads, and more, along with the current morning newspaper. The cowpokes of old never had it so good!

It may be that a few of the residents from former establishments are still hanging around, though, because apparitions have been reported in both the Cowboy room and the Cattleman's room. Vicki Isaacs, one of the founders of Metroplex Paranormal Investigations, told me that the Cowboy was one of the locations where her group found supernatural activity.

The Cowboy room is decorated in the style of an old bunkhouse from the period when cowpokes drove cattle to the

Stockyards. It has twin iron beds and even a potbelly stove in the corner of the room. Items such as a saddle, spurs, branding irons, and tack complete the decor. The folks at Miss Molly's fashioned this room as a tribute to the many cowhands who passed through Fort Worth on their way up the Chisholm Trail.

One of the ladies who once inhabited what is now the Cowboy room seems to be lingering to this very day, however. A few visitors to the room have had the opportunity to awaken to see a beautiful young lady standing near the bed. The spirit exudes a feeling of comfort and peace, and when she finally vanishes, the guest has a feeling of sorrow to see her go. If the spirit is that of one of the working girls of the hotel's bawdy house days, she seems only to be stopping by for a tranquil visit to her old room.

Another reportedly haunted room is the Cattleman, which contains a large, carved oak queen bed below mounted longhorns. The décor is plush in this room, outfitted in the style that one of the cattle barons of old would be accustomed to, complete with a longhorn hide wall-hanging. A specter also appears in this room, but this one is that of an older woman, dressed in turn-of-the-century clothing that includes an old-fashioned sunbonnet. No one knows for sure, but it is speculated that this might be Miss Amelia, looking in to see how things are going at her old boardinghouse.

The purpose behind either one of these appearances is unclear, but other things seem to happen throughout the hotel. Metroplex Paranormal Investigations found a strange shadow in Miss Josie's room that they were able to capture on film, along with some activity in front of one of the hall bathrooms.

Typical haunting occurrences also are reported at Miss Molly's. When things are quiet and the guests have either stepped out for a while or turned in for the evening, the sound of footsteps have been heard in the hall, when no earthly visitor is there. Another manifestation is the sudden chill of the air, in an isolated spot, that seems to be just floating around the floor. Lights have also been known to turn on or off by themselves, and doors have been found open when they were last closed by human hands. Maybe Miss Amelia does return occasionally, just to shut a door here or turn off a light there. If she made similar inspections during the period when the hotel was a brothel, then there's no doubt the old hostess must be ecstatic with the way Miss Molly's has been transformed into the lovely bed and breakfast that it is today.

Miss Molly's Bed & Breakfast
109½ W. Exchange Avenue
Fort Worth, TX 76106
Phone: 817.626.1522
Fax: 817.625.2723
Toll Free: 1-800-99 MOLLY
Web: http://www.missmollys.com/

# The Phantom Figures of the Old Spaghetti Warehouse

Sitting on a hill overlooking the Fort Worth Stockyards is the brightly colored Spaghetti Warehouse. I've enjoyed their Italian cuisine on several previous trips to the Stockyards, but when I visited there for the purpose of writing this book I was on a ghost-hunting outing and looking for a little more than a plate of their delicious pasta. Okay, okay, I was probably going to indulge myself in a plate of fettuccini before all things were said and done, but I'd found an article in the Wednesday, October 31, 2001 edition of the TCU *Daily Skiff* that indicated the restaurant might have a haunted side to it, so I parked my car in the Stockyards and climbed the hill to the Spaghetti Warehouse.

Now, one of the myths about the place is that it used to be a brothel, and Lord knows, in its heyday, the Stockyards certainly had its share. To this tale, however, I cry "Bull!" and mean it literally. The fact is that the building was originally the Administration Building of the Swift and Company meat packing plant.

The story about how an Illinois company found its way down to the very heart of the Old West in Texas is a very interesting one

indeed. It is a tale with both hope and tragedy, and it begins over one hundred years ago.

Swift and Company was founded in Chicago back in the 1880s by a man named Gustavus Franklin Swift, who is also credited with inventing the refrigerated railway car. His invention would later prove to be a factor in the downfall of his company in the stockyards, but for now, just hang on to that fact and enjoy the story.

Although it was doing very well in Chicago, the company was lured to Fort Worth by a gentleman named Greenlief W. Simpson, who had purchased the Fort Worth Union Stockyards in 1893 and wanted to establish a central point of focus for the cattle business. He offered more money per head than the rival Kansas City live-stock market and was instantly flooded with ranchers shipping their cattle to Fort Worth. Greenlief therefore needed a packer who could process the meat and ship it throughout the country.

The city of Fort Worth also knew that large businesses would be good for the economy, so the city fathers joined with Simpson to bring in two of the nation's largest meat packing giants, Swift and Company and Armour and Company. The companies were offered subsidies, land for their huge plants, and even a part ownership in the Stockyards itself to relocate their businesses to Texas. In 1902 the final agreements were reached, and Swift and Company opened its doors in March of 1904 during Fort Worth's annual Fat Stock Show. In only a few years' time, the cattle drives that once went to the Midwest were now stopping in Fort Worth, making it one of the largest livestock markets in the nation. Times were good, and both the Swift and Armour companies were enjoying prosperity.

One of the buildings in the Swift and Company plant was the stately and massive Administration Building, positioned up on a hill above the stock pen, and it was here that the normal business of the company was conducted on a daily basis.

For many years the cattle were taken from the trail drives and then later from the trains and sold at auction right there in the Stockyards to the highest bidder. Of course, the winning bid was usually placed by either the Swift or Armour Company.

As transportation flourished across the country, however, the stockyards business took a downturn. The extent of the railroad to all parts of the country and the advent of refrigerated railway cars—remember, Swift himself invented these—meant that meat packing could be done at local livestock auctions and feedlots, and therefore the need for one centralized packing center slowly faded. By 1962 Armour and Company had closed its doors, and things weren't faring much better for Swift.

When it looked as if Swift and Company would close up shop as well, their workers took a pay cut to try to keep the plant open. They did the same thing in 1969, hoping to save Swift and the four-teen hundred employees that depended on it for a livelihood. As much as they tried, nothing could save the plant, and in 1971 it shut down its operation in the stockyards. A fire swept through the remains of the plant in the mid-seventies, leaving only the Admin-istrative Office sitting up on the hill.

Today the office building has been turned into one of the best Italian eateries in Fort Worth, still standing there, facing the ruins of what once was the Swift plant.

I wrote up all of this from my notes while waiting on my entrée among the stained glass lamps and trophy bucks, but I wondered exactly what spirits might be lurking within the walls. All I'd actually heard was that there was some kind of fire in the building, and a woman was killed before it could be controlled. It was supposedly her spirit that hadn't left yet and was occasionally seen standing in a window when the building was empty and locked.

Some folks there don't really have any details about the ghost, but I am fortunate enough to be able to pass along a few stories from a former manager of the Spaghetti Warehouse. First of all, the employees were always hearing strange noises, such as activity in a particular dining room that was not open. Just imagine yourself to be a waiter, passing by one of the rooms that you know isn't being used one evening, only to hear the moving of chairs and the scuffling of feet, but when you peer inside, there is not a single person there, and nothing is out of order. Very creepy, but these are the kinds of things that seem to happen all of the time.

Even more dramatic, however, was one particular evening when the manager was closing up and heard noises coming from the bar area. It was about two-thirty in the morning, and he thought he was the only one in the place, so he rushed downstairs to see what was going on. Sitting at the bar was the shadow-form of a man. Since it was obvious that the patron wasn't an earthly visitor, the manager quickly left the room. When he finally went back, before locking up, the presence was no longer there.

A second sighting of an apparition at the restaurant happened when he was leaving after closing the place, again, in the wee morning hours. He had just finished his "walk through," where he takes a look in every room to make sure things are in order then turns off the lights and continues on. Finding everything to be satisfactory, he set the alarm, locked the front doors, and walked out to his car. Something unexplainable made him stop and look back at the building, however, and standing there in a third floor window was a person looking directly down at him.

Was this the woman I'd heard about? Well, he couldn't discern whether the form was male or female, only that it was standing up there looking directly at him. There's no way that someone could have gotten inside without tripping the alarm, of course, so he just chalked the experience up to another strange occurrence there at the Spaghetti Warehouse.

While I was visiting, I didn't see or feel anything suspicious at all. There were no unearthly noises, no spectral forms like the former manager had seen, not even a cold spot on that warm spring day. All I knew for certain was that the food was exquisite, and I enjoyed every last bite I could hold. I asked that the rest be bundled up in a doggie bag for me to enjoy later.

Walking back down to the Stockyards, I did look back over my shoulder, but I saw no spirit standing in the windows. Maybe I was just there too early in the day or they didn't see fit to manifest themselves on that particular occasion. I was only a little disappointed, since I did have a sack with a few more spoonfuls of fettuccini to enjoy as soon as I got home.

Spaghetti Warehouse
600 E. Exchange Ave.
Fort Worth, TX 76106
Phone: 817.625.4171
Fax: 817.625.4174
Web: http://www.meatballs.com/

# The Ghosts of Garland

**T**he city of Garland was established to solve a problem. You see, two communities, named Duck Creek and Embree, had been fighting for some time over which one of them should have the regional post office.

Duck Creek felt they deserved the honor, because it was a station on the Missouri, Kansas and Texas Railroad. Embree believed it had just as much right, because it was a station on the Atchison, Topeka and Santa Fe Railroad.

The problem was solved in 1887, when Congressman Joseph Abbott sent a bill to Congress to locate a post office directly between the two towns. A community was established there and named for President Grover Cleveland's attorney general, Augustus H. Garland.

This city had two distinctions for me while researching this book: one of the most interesting cases, and one of the most disappointing.

The interesting aspect is one you'll read about in the Mills Cemetery story that follows. Not that it has the best tale of a haunting, but because it required the most detective work. It was great fun, and I felt like Columbo trying to solve a case!

I was disappointed, however, by another place concerning a very real spirit. I was able to locate and talk to someone who had experienced the ghost, and I was looking forward to writing the story. The location itself did not want to reveal the fact that it was haunted, and since they had never gone on public record as being such, I respected their wishes. Perhaps in a future book I'll be able to write about this place, but for the time being, I have to keep its confidence and remain silent. For now, know that there is a particular building within the city where many people walk every day, side by side, with one entity that is not among the living. You might have been there yourself!

# Mills Cemetery's Ghost of Smiley

I tend to be a little skeptical of haunted graveyard tales. You see, the spirits I've found tend to be in the places that meant something to them in life—or at the site of their death. Cemeteries are simply places where the earthly remains of humans are interred and usually not a location where a spirit would linger. The place probably wouldn't mean anything to them at all!

Still, there are many graveyard sites across our country where ghostly activity has been reported, especially those that are connected with battlefields. One North Texas cemetery I visited had no such distinction, however.

When I was doing research for this book, I used a three-prong approach to finding haunted places: newspaper, interviews, and the Internet. The truly haunted locations could be cross checked across all three, which gave the stories some validity. This particular burial ground came from an Internet lead, but since it didn't turn up in interviews or in any newspaper articles over the last twenty years, I was a little cynical. But I'm getting ahead of myself. Let me start at the beginning:

I ran across an Internet posting about something called "Smiley's Grave" in Garland. Most of the websites that mentioned it had the exact text that had been lifted from the same source. Basically, it said that a place called "Mills Cemetery" was haunted by a man named Smiley.

With a little research, I uncovered two different stories about the supposed haunting:

1) A man with the surname of "Smiley" slaughtered his entire family on one fateful night and then killed himself. The manifestation takes place at only one time of year. If you were to lie on his grave at midnight on Halloween, it would be difficult to

stand back up—if you could get back up at all. The ghost of Smiley is holding you down on his grave!

2)    A man named Smiley was killed in a shootout at his home with men he'd been quarreling with. It was the current equivalent to a drive-by, and the house was peppered with bullets. Not only was Mr. Smiley killed, but his entire family was also murdered by the assailants. Because of the agony of his family being murdered along with him, the husband walks through the cemetery at night. Park your car there, turn off the headlights, and perhaps you will see his ghost.

It all sounded a bit fishy, at best. Still, the fact that there was a story about the graveyard dictated a visit for the purposes of this book. I decided to call on the cemetery twice—once as the sun was setting, to get a flavor for the place at night, and another time in the early morning hours when I could get a good look around. Both times I walked respectfully among the tombstones, looking for any sign of "Smiley's grave," and remained open for any possible indication that I wasn't alone there.

Mills Cemetery was a quiet, peaceful place, with only the sound of an occasional automobile on the nearby highway or a passing songbird to break the silence. I walked along the paths, wondering about all these people—who they had been, what they had done for a living, and what life was like in Garland back when they were alive. Walking through a cemetery is always a humbling experience for me. It reminds me that no matter what our hopes and dreams are, no matter what we accomplish in life or how important we become, every single one of us has a date set to pass over to the other side. I have heard a few people say they make all of their important decisions while standing in a cemetery; it helps them to keep the proper perspective about things. All in all, not a bad idea.

After looking around some, I finally found Smiley's grave, a family headstone that must have been associated with a tragic story.

The Smiley family marker

The grave marker read:

SMILEY
Mother: Belle Hall, October 30, 1890
Father: Chas Oscar, March 17, 1890
Daughters:
Lilath Merle, June 20, 1914
Gretta May, October 27, 1915
Charlena, February 20, 1926
All Died May 9, 1927

As the tombstone said, the entire family had all died on the same day, from the thirty-seven-year-old father to the youngest daughter, only three months old. I guessed that either one of the tales I had heard could have been responsible for the mass burial of the family, but I'd be a very irresponsible ghost hunter to try to choose only between those two.

An event that could take the lives of an entire family would surely be newsworthy, so the next stop was at the Garland Public Library to search for clues; the process didn't take all that long. It didn't take much to discover that on May 9, 1927, a tornado destroyed much of the city of Garland and killed seventeen people, including a former Garland city mayor, S. E. Nicholson. That fact would easily explain the consecutive deaths of the family members and put to rest any stories of murders or gun battles.

Just to be thorough, however, I posted a message on a local Internet supernatural discussion group, hoping to get a reply that would resolve the legend one way or the other. As it turns out, I got several. All were from high school students, each one swearing that the stories of the ghost of Mills Cemetery were true. I corresponded with a couple, asking what had been seen and why they believe in the haunting so strongly.

The answer? Because they went to the cemetery on a date, and it was creepy. Sigh.

In my mind, the Legend of Smiley's Grave is nothing more than a local story that is kept alive among the students of the area. Perhaps it is a rite of passage to visit the graveyard at night, or lay on one particular grave or another at Halloween, but there is no indication that there is more to it than that.

It is a little sad, in a way, because cemeteries are places where people come to pay respect to the memories of their loved ones. I think I'll go back, though, just one more time. I'll lay a bouquet of five roses on the Smiley family grave and hope they have all found peace after the terrible tragedy that befell them on that horrible day back in 1927.

Mills Cemetery
Garland, TX

# The Ghosts of Granbury

There was only one location in Granbury that I'd heard stories about, and in fact, it turned out to have a very healthy reputation for its ghost. Before getting into that, though, I have to mention that Granbury is the county seat of Hill County—just what is it with these places? Well, whatever the case, I guarantee that as I continue to look for ghosts, I'm going to be examining the county seats. It seemed like I visited them all in the course of writing this book!

The city was founded in 1854 by a diverse group of people, many from Tennessee. Tom Lambert and Amon Bond led a group from Tennessee, along with Elizabeth Crockett and family, also from Tennessee. And if her name sounds familiar, keep in mind she was settling land that had been awarded by the Republic of Texas to heirs of men who fought in the Texas Revolution in 1836. The town itself was named for General Hiram Bronson Granbury, a man who led the Confederate troops from this area during the Civil War.

It grew in commerce and trade, and almost a hundred years after it was formed, a dam was erected on the Brazos River at De Cordova Bend, just southeast of Granbury. Lake Granbury was formed, giving the residents a beautiful location for warm-weather water sports. The *Granbury Queen*, an old-style paddle wheel boat, still provides a beautiful lake cruise on weekends.

Visitors to the town are attracted to the historic old square, though, which leads right into our next haunted North Texas location, the Granbury Opera House.

# The Theater Ghost of the Granbury Opera House

It had been some time since I'd been to Granbury, and as I looked around, I wasn't sure I had ever visited the square. I had quite a surprise, though—the place was wonderful!

Now, I know I was ghost hunting, but I couldn't help but move along through some of the stores with the other visitors to the city. On that particular Saturday, there were quite a few people in town, and everyone seemed to be having a ball roaming from place to place.

The historic town square is ringed by shops that offer everything from local delicacies to hand-made crafts. And while I was in town, the visitors were enjoying each and every one. While trying to find my destination there in Granbury, I quickly discovered there are two theaters on the square, offering live entertainment to packed houses with every performance.

My business was at the Granbury Opera House, so I decided to follow the sidewalk around to the wonderful old building. I took a couple of photos then headed on inside. I've got to say that the place has been meticulously restored, but I didn't know the half of it until I'd done a little more investigation. I put the ghost quest on hold for a bit to get the background story on the theater.

I found out it was actually built way back in 1886, back in a time when the city of Granbury was considered to be part of the Texas frontier and not a location where many polite citizens dwelled. The rough trade of the town was fed by railroad workers and ranch hands, and so several saloons and gambling establishments took root. A bawdy house or two even existed to serve the transient men that worked in town.

The gentle folks of Granbury needed a dose of culture in such a rough environment, and so the son of a settler from South Carolina named Henry Kerr constructed the theater in 1886. Before too long, Kerr's Hall, as it was known back then, quickly became the center of activity in the town: traveling vaudeville acts, bands, magicians, minstrel shows, acrobats, and drama companies, all found a place to perform for the local citizens.

Not everyone shared the good feelings about the grand theater, however. Even though it was an attempt at culture in a rough and rugged time, some of the good citizens of the town saw the devil's hand in the stage productions there. After all, many of the plays were love stories, and the very idea of, heaven forbid, two unmarried people kissing on stage was positively shocking. Because of this, parents sometimes forbade the young people of the town from patronizing the theater, and in fact, some were not permitted to even walk on the south side of the square!

You'd think the theater wouldn't be all that scandalous, what with the saloons and brothels in close proximity. Maybe it was the fact that the theater was erected under the guise of culture and polite society that caused the problem, but for whatever reason, the place was not without its detractors.

There were as many supporters, however, and Henry Kerr eventually enlarged the theater's stage and brought in backdrops to enhance the performances: professionally painted drops, and even four full stage curtains.

I'm taking a side-trip away from ghosts for a minute, because I'd be horribly remiss in my duties if I wrote about the Granbury Opera House without mentioning one of its most famous—or perhaps notorious—employees: John St. Helen.

Mr. St. Helen took bit roles at the Opera House and poured drinks at a bar next to the theater. He was a teetotaler, however, never imbibing in alcohol…except for one particular day every year: April 14. On that day he would drink himself into an annual stupor. No one knew why, and the gentleman himself wouldn't expound on it.

Mr. St. Helen had a cousin who lived in the area, and rumor had it he had begged her to keep from revealing her maiden name. Secrets can't be kept in a small town, though, and it was learned that the lady had been named Fannie Booth.

The final piece to the puzzle didn't fall into place until the day Mr. St. Helen was set to pass away. There on his deathbed, he revealed to a few close friends that the name John St. Helen was manufactured. In actuality, his name was John Wilkes Booth, the man who had assassinated President Abraham Lincoln on April 14, 1865. He even went as far as to tell them the murder weapon could be found wrapped in newspaper, hidden behind the boards of a house that he specified.

Now, conventional history dictates that the manhunt for John Wilkes Booth culminated by him being killed in a tobacco barn in Virginia on April 26, 1865, so his confession was a startling development. It might have all ended there, but something else happened to complicate the story even further: Mr. St. Helen got better.

His secret finally told, Mr. St. Helen (or Booth, as the case may be) fled the small city of Granbury, never to return. The story became local legend, and a gun was found exactly where he'd said it would be, wrapped in an old newspaper bearing headlines about the presidential assassination.

Whether Mr. St. Helen was actually John Wilkes Booth is a topic that may never die. Conclusive evidence has been found for both sides of the argument, and people are completely unyielding in their opinions. Read more about it in *Return of Assassin John Wilkes Booth* by W.C. Jameson.

The only thing certain is that John St. Helen took the role of an occasional actor at the theater and poured liquor at the saloon next door.

As it turns out, saloons such as that one helped to bring the downfall of the theater. More Granbury legend comes into play as the temperance crusader Carrie A. Nation rolled into town in 1911, with her famous hatchet that had hacked up the doors of drinking establishments across the country. The story goes that she chopped up seven different saloons on the square and whipped the local people into a frenzy of righteousness. The saloons were closed down, and the theater, with its reputation that had already offended some in town, shut its doors as well.

The once-grand theater was abandoned, and portions of the building served briefly as various businesses such as a grocery store, bowling alley, then a doctor's office, an insurance agency, and an abstract company. The old girl was falling into perpetual ruin, until it eventually consisted of little more than four stone walls. It changed hands several times, but on September 29, 1972, was deeded to Joe L. Nutt, a man whose ancestors had figured significantly in the history of Granbury. He then sold the building to the newly formed Opera House Association for the small sum of sixteen thousand dollars. The association acquired the building on August 28, 1974.

The half-million-dollar restoration of the Opera House was done entirely with private money, under the direction of Jo Ann Miller. Ms. Miller not only oversaw the operation but also stayed on as its first managing director, serving for twenty-one years. After the theater stage had been dark for over six decades, the Granbury Opera House opened its doors to the public once again on June 19, 1975, with a production of *Gold in the Hills*, directed by Jo Ann Miller herself. The theater company has been playing to capacity crowds ever since that day and is a major attraction on the square.

I first learned about the haunting in the Granbury Opera House while reading a book by Joan Upton Hall and Stacey Hasbrook, a fascinating exploration of historic theaters across the state named *Grand Old Texas Theaters That Won't Quit*. In their book, Joan Upton Hall recounts a conversation with the current managing director, Mary Van Kleek. "Van Kleek told me in June 2001 that the latest thing going on is that a group is coming to research the resident ghost." She also said you can hear footsteps pacing in the balcony quite frequently, and those who have actually seen the ghost describe him as wearing a white shirt, dark pants, and tall, heavy boots.

The spirit isn't one to be feared, however. The extent of his mischief at the Granbury Opera House includes moving props from the current production and playing with the lights and doors.

I set out to find the group who had investigated the theater and located Metroplex Paranormal Investigations. I contacted Vicki Isaacs, one of the founders of the group, and asked what had inspired them to check out the Granbury Opera House. Vicki told me, "Actually, another investigator got the contact information and wasn't really interested in going out there so he passed it along to me. At the time we were a new group and thought it was really cool that we got to go out there and spend the night. Come to think of it, it's still pretty cool." I have to concur—it sounds like a wonderful opportunity.

"After interviewing several of the actors," Vicki went on to say, "there were a couple of places thought to be more active than others, such as the stage area and the 'shoe' room in the costume shop." During their stay there, some members of the group observed lights that came on and went off again without any human assistance. The most interesting thing was that some of these lights had been unplugged by members of the investigation team, yet they turned on anyway. Some photographic anomalies occurred as well, which are published on the group's website, www.metroplexparanormalinvestigations.com.

No one seems to know who the spirit is that haunts the Opera House, but between those happenings and the stories about John Wilkes Booth having worked there, the Granbury Opera House is a very interesting place indeed and certainly warrants a visit. While you're there, be sure to take in the show, but get your tickets early; the place sells out to its human visitors very quickly!

Granbury Opera House
116 E. Pearl St.
Granbury, TX 76048

# The Ghosts of Hillsboro

Hillsboro is yet another county seat. This is getting very inter-esting; could every county seat be haunted? Who knows? There is certainly one place in Hillsboro that has a few interesting things going on, though, and I'm extremely glad I found it.

This quaint city was established back in 1881 and was a center of commerce for Hill County. The downtown area is built in a typi-cal town-square fashion around a stately old 1874 courthouse. The courthouse was a beautiful structure, and I even have a painting inspired by it hanging in my home. January 1, 1993, was a devas-tating day for the county. The historic courthouse building burned to the ground due to faulty electrical wiring. Only its walls remained, leaving a ghostly shell standing in the town square; the roof and clock tower were both completely destroyed. The town rallied around its courthouse, though, and Hill County native Willie Nelson even performed at a benefit to raise funds for the restoration of the building.

The town square is once again a majestic place, boasting a completely restored courthouse. I just love that story and greatly enjoy visiting there. When I was doing research for this book, it was a genuine pleasure to learn that I'd be going to Hillsboro again.

I didn't count on the wonderful bed and breakfast I found there, though, which just made the town even better. It's just a few blocks off the town square, and so I'll quit talking about court-houses and get on with the story of the spirits of the Tarlton House.

# Tarlton House—A B&B
# Between Dimensions

In the introduction to this book, I said my goal was to always keep learning. Well, I've got to tell you, I learned something new while sitting out on the front porch of the Tarlton House Bed and Breakfast one pleasant morning in May. Or, at least I came away with something new to contemplate.

My host, Pat Lovelace, had just taken me on a tour of the house with its bay windows, lion-footed tubs, and exquisite armoires. Pat had given me many wonderful stories about its history and the supernatural things people had seen there, and we were pretty much wrapping up the morning.

We walked through eight plush rooms, all lavishly decorated and inviting. One of my favorites was up on the third floor, the Gables Suite, so named because it is tucked up among the gables of the house. It was spacious, yet cozy at the same time. The

Tower suite was the same way, and quite honestly, I'd have trouble choosing between the two.

Usually, when I'm picking a room at a bed and breakfast, I look at my choices on the B&B's Internet web page (and in this case, you should definitely check out www.tarltonhouse.com). Once I get a feel for the rooms, I'll call up the inn to find out what's available on the nights I plan on being there, which sometimes narrows my selection down some. Finally, I always ask where the latest supernatural activity has been occurring. In the case of the Tarlton House, though, the selection isn't that difficult: Any of the rooms there would be a magnificent choice, and as for the ghosts, well, things have happened all over the bed and breakfast. That makes this particular inn a great stop for those seeking a "spirited" stay during a getaway.

The subject of the nature of ghosts came up as we sat in the rockers out on the porch, and after I told her some of the things I'd heard, Pat caught me completely off guard. "Not that I don't believe in the possibility of spirits," she said, "but I think there is more of a scientific explanation for the things that happen at the Tarlton House." I was fascinated as she went though some of the possibilities, but then, I'm getting ahead of myself. To contemplate the things that happen at the Tarlton House, you first have to understand how it came to be.

The home was built back in 1895 by a family named Tarlton, who came to Texas from Louisiana and settled in the Hillsboro area. The husband, Greene Duke Tarlton, was a title attorney and first built a land and title office in 1892 on Franklin Street. When his business took off he had the house constructed for his family.

Over the next few years, their family had grown to five children, and things were going very well for the Tarltons. Mrs. Tarlton became known throughout the area for the musical events that she held at the house, which included singing and piano playing into the wee morning hours. In fact, the family owned one of the first baby grand pianos in Hillsboro. An elderly lady from the town told Mrs. Lovelace that she still remembered Mrs. Tarlton singing a special with one of her daughters in church.

Mrs. Tarlton had trouble seeing in her later years, and her husband had tile installed in the house with raised patterns so that she could still enjoy the furnishings. With her eyesight failing, she died in 1907, perhaps from complications of diabetes, which would explain the vision problems. The entire town grieved for her loss, and a loving inscription was placed on her tombstone:

The World Is At Loss Without Her Voice

From all indications, Mr. Tarlton was heartbroken. As Pat Lovelace told me, "For the next five years, the kids ruled the roost. People have told me stories about roller skating in the hallways of the old house back when they were children." It's not hard to imagine, though. During my tour of the bed and breakfast, Pat showed me the upstairs rooms, which at one time had pretty much been open attic where the children could play.

The joviality in the house stopped in 1913, though, when Mr. Tarlton took a new bride. The kids apparently didn't like her either because they thought she was taking the place of their mother, or for whatever other reason. The rift was apparently so large that Tarlton built another house beside his original one for him and his new wife. The children remained in the old house with the governess, and that seemed to resolve the issue. When one of his daughters married, Mr. Tarlton gave them some land on the other side of the original house for a home of their own.

Once again, things were rocking along for the family, when another tragedy befell them in 1929. During the great stock market crash, Greene Duke Tarlton lost most of his money and financial holdings. He was forced to sell off everything, including the lands he owned in Texas and Oklahoma.

Two years later, in 1931, an event occurred that would shake the very foundations of the family. The second Mrs. Tarlton took ill and died of pneumonia. Her obituary concluded with the solitary line:

Mr. Tarlton died the same day.

It took Pat Lovelace some time to get the actual truth as to what happened on that fateful day, but she finally learned that

Greene Tarlton was overcome with grief and depression, and with his finances depleted, his tolerance for such things had just been worn down. He climbed the stairs of the original home, the Tarlton House Bed and Breakfast of today, and hung himself on the third floor. He was seventy-one years old.

His was a sad tale, with a horrific end that most innkeepers might hesitate to tell, but Ms. Lovelace is quick to share it with her guests. You see, it is because of the suicide that the house exists today.

After some time the houses began to fall into ruin—the original house, along with the daughter's house beside it. The doors were left open in the hopes that intruders wouldn't break the windows to get inside. The daughter's house was ransacked and damaged beyond repair; it finally had to be razed. The original Tarlton house was spared, however. Everyone knew about the legendary hanging, and so few lingered inside; they were terrified about whatever ghosts might occupy the site of such a tragic event. Since few would even set foot inside the house—and those who did ran quickly back out—the windows and the structure itself are still intact.

But the house is not without its spirits. Pat told me, "Footsteps happen all the time. You hear them, but no one is there." Her sister-in-law happened to be visiting when I was there, and she'd come in as a confirmed skeptic. While alone in the house, she heard steps in a hallway and realized that the stories about the Tarlton House must be true.

Pat herself has many stories about the events in the house. She was on the third floor making up the room known as Abby's Attic, which is a beautiful upstairs room with floral print walls and a plush blue carpet. The room not only has a king-sized bed, but also has a bed in an alcove, which she had to put her knee on to lean over and adjust the air conditioning. As she did, she felt a heavy push on the bed beside her knee, as if someone had just sat down on the edge. Pat initially thought it was her cat, but when she couldn't find the feline anywhere, she realized that someone else had been there—someone she was unable to see. In the months

Abby's Attic, where Pat Lovelace had a ghostly experience

that followed, many guests reported an unseen presence sitting down on the bed next to them.

One such guest was traveling with her husband, who got up early one morning for a day trip. As the wife slept in for the day, she felt someone sit down on the far side of the bed, and she thought it was very romantic for her husband to come back upstairs to kiss her goodbye. When no kiss came, she rolled over and saw that no one was in the room with her—she was alone.

Still, everything that happens at the Tarlton House is very gentle, nonintrusive, and benevolent. A few guests have even seen Mr. Tarlton upstairs, bending over, as if to reach down to his children. A woman's voice has also been heard gently singing in the house, which of course, is probably that of Mrs. Tarlton. Children have also been heard laughing on the third floor, the place where they used to play.

These kinds of things have led Pat Lovelace to an interesting conclusion—that these aren't ghosts, but are instead a folding of another dimension over onto our own. As I said earlier, she doesn't

The Living Room of the Tarlton House

discount the possibilities of ghosts by any classic definition, but the things that happen at the Tarlton house seem to be unaffected by the present-day world, as if they were simply scenes being replayed from a past time. She talked to me about Steven Hawking and his theories about the past, present, and future all bleeding between each other. I have to say, it makes as much sense as any of the other theories about ghosts, so maybe there is something to it. When Mr. Tarlton is seen up on the third floor, it could be that he is in his own time, leaning down to play with his kids, and that image is occasionally visible today. After all, the third floor was where the children played, and the scene would have been very natural when he was alive. The same could be said for Mrs. Tarlton's singing and the sounds of the children playing; they could be remnants of a past time that happen to be fading into ours momentarily. When I left Tarlton House and headed back to my car, I did so promising myself to pick up one of Steven Hawking's books just to see what he has to say.

That way, when I come back I might be a little more prepared in case something happens—and I will be back. The inn is luxurious, the accommodations plush, and I'd love to spend an evening out on that front porch, just watching the world drift by.

Tarlton House
211 N. Pleasant St.
Hillsboro, TX 76645
Toll Free: 1.800.823.7216
Web: http://www.tarltonhouse.com

Text of the State of Texas Historical Marker assigned to Tarlton House:

### Old G.D. Tarlton House
Victorian Style. Built in 1895 by noted attorney Greene Duke Tarlton (1852-1931), from Louisana.

House was one of finest in town, with hand-carved mantels, stained glass windows, "speaking tube" between kitchen and third floor bedroom, and a dumbwaiter. Cistern on back porch supplied cool water all year round.

Outbuildings included stable and coach house. On grounds were grape arbor, orchard, and garden. Restored by Dana L. Bennett. Recorded Texas Historic Landmark - 1972

# The Ghosts of Mansfield

I found Mansfield, Texas, to be the home of the legendary Hatchet Man Bridge. Where was this bridge of local high school tales? I don't know; I certainly couldn't find it! I had originally thought it might be over Walnut Creek, which runs through the town and is pretty much responsible for the founding of the city.

Two men, Ralph S. Man from South Carolina and Julian B. Feild from Virginia, had settled in Fort Worth and were partners in the milling business. In 1857, though, the pair sold their sawmill and gristmill and moved a little further south to an area known for its production of wheat. They saw a lucrative potential for business, and so they built a sawmill and the first steam-powered gristmill in the county, possibly even the state. A settlement grew up around the mills and was named for the two men, Man and Feild. The original spelling of the town name was Mansfeild, but it changed over time to its current designation.

Driving around Mansfield, there was never any indication of such a place, nor was I able to find any directions at the stops I made there. Hatchet Man was a secondary consideration for me, though, because I had another destination in town. Although I never did find Hatchet Man Bridge, or much of anything about it, I had been lucky enough to discover a jewel while I was there: a historic place named the Farr Best Theater.

# The Mischievous Ghost of the Farr Best Theater

Traveling along the main drag that goes through Mansfield, Highway 287/157, you might notice the Main Street Theatre as you pass through town. With a casual glance, you might even miss this historic old place, but if that happened, you'd be doing yourself a great disservice.

When I visited Mansfield, the Main Street Theatre had a production of *Damn Yankees* playing, and with that combination of the Devil and professional baseball, I knew it was going to be extremely hard to pass the performance up to stay on my ghost hunting schedule that day.

On the top of the theater's marquee are the words "Farr Best," and if you didn't know what they meant, you might not give them a second thought. Much history is contained in those two words, though, both of Mansfield and of the theater itself.

I came to learn that the theater was named for—and by—a Mr. Milton Farr, but as it turns out he had nothing to do with the spirit that dwells in the old place. Instead, he provided the backdrop for a ghost that sort of "moved in" somewhere along the line.

Mr. Farr came to Mansfield all the way back in 1917 and at the time was one of the town's most influential citizens. A man with a vision, he oversaw the installation of the first electric lights in the city and a water system that was very modern for the times. As a patron of the arts, he also founded a motion picture house on which he hung the moniker, the "Farr Best Theater." And perhaps it was; with all of its modern conveniences of the time, it probably was the "far best" in all of the area! The theater opened its doors on the evening of October 10, 1917.

Farr's new lighting and water systems caught on in town, as you might expect, and so did the theater. In fact, it had such a long run that it was Mansfield's only movie theater until its last proprietor, Roy Farr, passed away in 1975. Still, there were no reports of ghosts or hauntings in the old place. Those came later.

Upon the death of Roy Farr, the building was sold to Charlotte Martin, who renamed it "The Old Bijou Theatre" and had hopes of continuing it as a motion picture house. She did just that, in fact, and the theater operated for five more years, until it was put up for sale again in 1980. Still, during all this time, there were no tales of ghosts associated with the place.

The next owner was St. John's Lutheran Church, which met at the theater for eight years. When the congregation opened the doors to their new facility, the Farr Best building was once again on the market in 1988. This time a local theater group named "Main Street Theatre, Inc." purchased the property. The theater company was formed on the idea of being an all-volunteer, nonprofit community theater group dedicated to bringing quality, live comedy, musical, and drama productions to Mansfield. And that they did.

Somewhere along the way during their ownership, though, a spirit made its presence known. Strange things began to happen in the theater. Lights flipped on and off, even though no one was near the controls, items disappeared, only to reappear again after everyone had searched the building, and other mischievous occurrences caused the staff to believe that something unseen was there.

From all accounts, it was a good-natured spirit, one that just seemed to play a few pranks every now and then, so the actors and staff assigned a name to the entity: McDougal.

One of the theater's volunteers, Beth Steele, gave a few thoughts on the subject to the *Arlington Morning News* for their October 25, 1996 issue: "McDougal came to the theater when Damon Steele donated part of a Scottish pub as a concession stand. With the pub came the ghost. It causes no harm, but wreaks small mischief only on occasion. If anything gets missing, we blame it on McDougal!"

As a nod to its original founder, the theater was renamed the Farr Best Theater on September 13, 1996, and it was declared a historic site.

The theater as it stands today

If McDougal is that quiet a spirit, then the average theatergoer might never know he's there. While it still might be a mystery as to why he moved in with the concession stand and why he is lingering there today, the fact remains that he couldn't have picked a better place to haunt. Even the most seasoned of Broadway actors will tell you that the heart and soul of the collective stage is found in local theater, so McDougal has found a wonderful place in the Farr Best. After all, he got to see their interpretation of *Damn Yankees*, and I had to miss it; but that's all right. I'll be back for one of their other productions!

Main Street Theatre
107 N. Main
Mansfield, TX 76063
Phone: 817.473.6060
Fax: 817.473.6611
Web: http://www.mainstreettheatre.org/

# The Ghosts of Milford

**I** only found one haunted location in the city of Milford, but man, was it a doozy! Not only does the bed and breakfast have a few friendly ghosts, but it is one of the most delightful places I visited while putting this book together. I think one of the most attractive things about the place was the second-story front porch, which overlooks downtown Milford, a sleepy little community with lots of character. When I return there, I'm going to sit out there on the porch just as soon as dusk sets in and watch the slow, small-town life closing down for the day.

The city itself started in the early 1850s, when several families came to the Mill Creek valley and purchased land there. In 1854 the town was laid out just south of the creek, and the name Milford was chosen by one of the founders, after a small town near Boston, Massachusetts. I also heard the name came from a place to cross in Mill Creek—a ford—hence the name Milford, but how towns actually get their names is often the cause of arguments. However it got its name, things started cropping right up: a general store, a schoolhouse that doubled as church, and a gristmill. The town officially incorporated in 1888.

Cotton was king in Milford back in those days. The railroad reached the town in 1890, making it the central shipping point for the area's many cotton farmers. There was a sudden explosion of commerce. In just a few years, there were three churches, two cotton gins, necessary businesses such as a bank and hotel, and various other stores to serve the ever-increasing population. The Texas Presbyterian College for Women located there in 1902, something that will factor into the haunted location when we start talking about it shortly.

The Great Depression hit Milford hard, though, and the town never quite recovered. The college closed down, many businesses folded, and by 1968 the town had reached its low point of population.

Strategically located between Hillsboro and Waxahachie, the city's growth has slowly climbed, however, as people are starting to rediscover its small-town charm. Whether you're looking for a place to live or simply a chance to get away for a weekend, give Milford a try; I fell in love with it. And the best introduction to Milford you'll find is at the Baroness Inn.

# The Young Ladies of the Baroness Inn

Walk through the front door of the Baroness Inn, and you're going to get a hug. Evelyn's just that kind of hostess. You'll quickly find that you're at home in the Baroness Inn, lavishly decorated in Victorian elegance. It didn't always look like that, though.

While driving through the small Texas town of Milford, an old, abandoned building caught the eye of Evelyn Williams. Love at first sight tends to supersede trespassing laws, so she parked her car and waded right into the ruins of the long-forgotten building. While everyone else saw broken glass, fallen timbers, and a building that bordered on being condemned, Evelyn was already decorating her inn and planning the first breakfasts for her guests.

She told me that her mother always said, "Honey, you can do anything you set your mind to." That lady must have been right, because after I saw the photos of the building in its state when Evelyn purchased it, I realized it would take someone with an incredible vision and dedication to turn the place into something that was even habitable, much less a beautiful inn that would attract visitors to the charming little town of Milford, Texas.

But Evelyn worked her magic, even though the renovation and restoration would be a five-year process. During that time, little things started to happen here and there that made her think something unusual was occurring at her inn.

In Evelyn's own words, "Apparently things were going on during the five years of remodeling, and we just did not realize what was causing it. In the beginning these were just annoying circumstances that kept repeating. I was in the midst of getting everything done, and we found that we just had no explanation for the incidents. I had so much going on at the time I didn't give them very much thought, except they *just kept happening*! It wasn't until these things started occurring with my guests that I began to realize we were dealing with something more than just circumstances." She cited some specific examples of the strange phenomenon to me: "My home had to have five years of extensive remodeling. I know you've been around construction sites enough to know how contractors will turn the radio up loud so they can hear it wherever they are in the building. It was during this process that the radio would all of a sudden switch stations. At first they thought one of their group might have changed it and kind of let it ride and started fussing at one another to quit changing the station. They would then find out that no one was touching the radio. They became spooked at one particular time when everyone was working all together and the radio in the hall switched stations. The workers looked at one another, put it back to country western music, and went back to work; then the radio changed the station again. At that point they knew no one else was around. It scared them bad enough that they left the job site immediately. They had a talk with me to advise me they did not intend to work late evenings anymore."

The workers didn't have to be frightened, as it turns out. The spirits of the Baroness Inn, whoever they may be, are very friendly. Perhaps the events with the radio were just a little prank played on the men who were causing all the noise and commotion at the house.

Ms. Williams got a call during the course of the restoration from her neighbor. He said, "Evelyn, you might want to check the windows better; there were two open this morning as I was leaving for work." She told me she appreciated the fact that he was keeping an eye on the place, and he even went in to close them since he had a key for just such reasons. She received similar reports from other friends in the area, to the point where she called the person overseeing the work on the inn to make him aware of the problem. He told her, "It's the strangest thing. I've made a point of driving by every evening to make sure everything is locked up tight. Bedogged if I haven't driven by the very next morning and these two windows were up. I can't figure it out!"

As restoration continued, along with the mysterious happenings in the building, Evelyn started doing research on its history. She soon found out it had been the girl's dorm for the Presbyterian Girls College. In 1850 Texas Presbyterian College put out a request for bids for a home for its school for girls. The city of Milford made an offer that was accepted by the college: ten acres of land and $25,000 cash. To build the dormitory, the bricks for the walls were made on the property itself, and the cypress wood for the heavy structural beams was hauled in from Louisiana by oxen. The Texas Presbyterian School for Girls opened in Milford, and the dormitory housed thirty-one people: twenty-two students and nine faculty members.

Some years later the college moved to Sherman, and the building became a hotel for the city of Milford. From there it had a stint as a boardinghouse before it was abandoned and started falling into ruins—and started its wait for Evelyn.

Once her restoration was complete and the bed & breakfast was open, the spirits became a little bolder, actually appearing to a few couples that were chosen—for whatever reason—for a visit from the other side. Keep in mind that the ghosts who occasionally show up at the Baroness Inn are gentle and benevolent; they seem to be young ladies who are reaching out to the living.

Evelyn told me about one couple who was attending the Murder Mystery weekend at the Baroness Inn. While everyone was telling ghost stories, the husband laughed at the very idea of ghosts. As everyone retired for the evening, he decided to sit out on the second-story back porch for a little while longer, and his wife retired to Lady Roxanne's Room. This particular upstairs room is decorated in warm colors, with a huge canopied pine bed and a private bath that features a corner marble Jacuzzi tub for two and a pedestal sink from 1900, making it a wonderful selection for a stay at the Baroness.

As the gentleman sat outside, relaxing and staring out at the evening stars, he felt a gentle hand touch his shoulder. The man was sure it was his wife who'd come outside from their room. He smiled and turned his head, only to find that he was alone out there on the porch. That incident made a believer out of him!

Another encounter with one of the spirits happened to a female guest who was staying with her husband in the Baroness' Room, which not only has a luxurious four poster bed with a canopy of white lace and flowers, but also a marble Jacuzzi tub surrounded by beveled mirrors and Corinthian marble columns. Believe me, this is one of the most romantic rooms in the entire inn.

Anyway, Evelyn provided me with an account of the experience there in the guest's own words. "My husband and I had spent some time laughing in the Jacuzzi tub, which for no apparent reason started jetting water up into the air, soaking the ceiling, mirrors, and walls of the room. We had turned the jets on and off twice before it finally worked correctly. We had arrived very late, and I was tired. We barely said goodnight to Evelyn and tried the

The main hallway downstairs, and the stairway
where footsteps have been heard

tub before bed. That night I didn't sleep well—tossing and turning
for some time before falling asleep. I woke up about 2:00 in the
morning, because I was freezing cold. I thought my husband had
stolen my covers, but they were tucked up to my chin. I must have
been gripping them in the night. Settling back to sleep, I heard a
woman's voice whispering. It was barely audible, but she seemed
to be instructing me on 'how to lace up my boots.' She mentioned
'pulling up my stockings' then tying by 'drawing the laces tight.' At
that moment it dawned on me that someone was *talking* to me. I
poked my husband, but he just rolled over. I sat up for many minutes, but nothing more happened. The room temperature seemed
to go back to normal. In the morning my husband remembered me
trying to wake him, but he never heard anything."

That wasn't the only occurrence in the Baroness' Room, however. Another couple was spending the night there and were in the
Jacuzzi tub together. They happened to glance back at the bed, and
sitting on the edge was a young lady in her early twenties, just

staring at them. As they watched, she slowly disappeared before their eyes. The couple threw on clothes, quickly packed, and ran down the stairs and knocked on Evelyn's door. They told her they were leaving immediately, but she finally calmed the pair down and convinced them to accompany her back up to the room. When she opened the door, she saw that the imprint of someone's bottom was clearly visible on the side of the bed. The couple swore it was exactly where the girl had been sitting, and that neither of them had gone near the bed since her appearance. The couple finally agreed to stay the rest of the night, but Evelyn told me, "I don't think they were ever really comfortable."

The bed where the ghostly young lady was sitting, and
the tub where the couple were when they first saw her.
Photo courtesy of the Baroness Inn

I was very comfortable when I visited the Inn, though. When you stay there, be sure to get directions to the old cemetery, where you can literally spend hours examining the ancient headstones. Evelyn can also point you to the hanging tree, where justice was dispensed with a rope many years ago in Milford. The Baron was hanged there, which brings up a town legend of a lady who was the namesake for the Inn: The Baroness.

Evelyn explained the legend of the Baroness quite well: "She looked every inch *the Baroness* that day in 1893 when her carriage drove into Milford. Her gown, deep cranberry velvet with satin trim, perfectly complimented her platinum hair. Her hat added another foot to her already tall and shapely frame. It was made with yards and yards of organza and had deep pink ostrich feathers flowing in all directions. The sun shining through the pink feathers of her hat made her look as though she was descending from the clouds into their little town. All the people in this tiny cotton mill town stopped and stared! Even the wealthy cotton merchants who did business in town were impressed. They knew they were seeing someone very special!

"She and the Baron stayed at the only hotel in town—the building that today is the Baroness Inn—and soon she was hosting elaborate parties for the cotton farmers and making the ladies in town feel special at her teas! It seemed as if she made the entire town feel special and alive. Even after the Baron left she continued to be the grand hostess. She explained that the Baron told her to wait right there while he attended to some pressing business. She knew he would come back, but in the meantime she had the philosophy of blooming where she was planted!"

The Baron did return, but the tables had turned somewhat. He had cheated several people in town and was quickly tried and executed down at the hanging tree.

While it doesn't seem to be the spirit of the Baroness that remains in the hotel, her taste for elegance and hospitality are well represented. It is a wonderful place and would be perfect for a romantic weekend. I'm not sure if I'm supposed to share this story, but Evelyn told me about one guest from the Metroplex who'd forgotten his wedding anniversary. He took off an hour or so early from work and drove down to the Inn to leave the luggage that he'd packed for himself and his wife. When he returned later that evening with his lovely lady, she was blindfolded, having been told that he was taking her to a secret getaway he'd been planning for their anniversary. (Married men, are you taking notes here?) They apparently enjoyed their stay there, never coming down from the second floor the entire weekend. Evelyn told me they were leaving food outside the door to the couple's room, and later they'd find the dirty dishes, so at least they knew they were still alive!

The porch at the Baroness Inn, overlooking Milford, Texas

As I was leaving the Baroness Inn, I asked Evelyn if she'd ever seen one of the ghosts. "No, but I've heard someone walking the upstairs hall. She paces from one end to the other, and I've found all the doors up there closed, even though I'd left them open on my last trip up. Another time, I was in bed and heard someone walking down the back stairs. The Inn was empty, so I knew what it had to be. I jumped up, and sure enough, there was no one there—at least, no one that I could see."

When I left the Inn, Evelyn had to give me a hug, because Evelyn's just that kind of hostess. You'll quickly find you're at home in the Baroness Inn.

The Baroness Inn
206 S. Main Street
Milford, TX 76670
Phone: 972.493.9393
Toll Free: 877.993.4924
Fax: 972.493.4626
Email: evelyn@baronessinn.com
Web: http://www.baronessinn.com

# The Ghosts of
# Mineral Wells

**B**efore I laid down the first few words of this book, I figured I'd include a few paragraphs about each city I visited. In this particular case, though, I ran into the problem of the town's history being an integral part of the ghost story I'm about to tell.

It's impossible to decouple the tale of the Baker Hotel with that of the town of Mineral Wells, so I'm not going to even try. You'll learn the interesting history of the city shortly, so I won't get into it here.

Suffice it to say, the city was built on its healing mineral waters, and during my visit I looked *everywhere* for a bottle to try. I never did find one, so if you have any idea how I can sample some of that medicinal liquid, please drop me an email; my address is at the end of the book. The magical elixir that came from the wells of this town so interested me I just have to try some!

One of the places that provided a haven for those flocking to Mineral Wells for health reasons was the Baker Hotel, arguably one of the most pampering resorts in the nation at the time. It was a little sad to see the Baker today, but then, I'm getting ahead of myself. Before I go too much farther, turn the page and let's get started on the hotel itself.

# The Health-Hunting Ghosts
# of the Baker Hotel

There's something in the water over in Mineral Wells. At least, that's what the town was banking on a little over a hundred years ago. When I started doing research on the town of Mineral Wells, both from a ghost aspect and a historical viewpoint, I was amazed. This was one of those places people flocked to for a miracle treatment for what ailed them—both the superstars of the day and the common folk alike.

The whole thing started when a gentleman named J.A. Lynch established a farm in the area in 1877, which was followed by a settlement a few years later. At the time, the railroad tracks only went as far as Millsap, Texas, so the road to the new town of Mineral Wells was covered by stagecoach. Occasionally there was a traveler or two on the coach, and when they climbed down for a drink of cool water at Mr. Lynch's stop, they found that the taste of the liquid from his well was extremely bitter. Many thought it tasted so bad it might be poison, in fact!

Lynch assured the folks that the water was safe to drink and went as far as to say that ingesting it had completely cured his rheumatism. A seed was planted in the travelers' minds, and a few people came back, citing some medicinal benefits after drinking the bad-tasting water. The legend of Mineral Wells was born. Of course the story went on, and in actuality, the acrid mineral water was both the rise and fall of the town.

When I heard that some supernatural activity had been reported at a hotel there, I decided to look further into the town's history. After all, if I was going to be visiting, I wanted to know what to expect.

Mineral Wells was about as far west as this book goes, and I can't say it wasn't a little bit of a haul out there that day. Still, there was something intriguing about my destination: The Baker Hotel. I'd heard tell you can see the skyscraper from some distance away, so I kept my eyes peeled on my westward drive.

As I drove, I reviewed my notes, which contained some pretty interesting things. I found out that by 1885, Mineral Wells was enjoying a genuine explosion in popularity due to the health benefits of its water that were being touted nationwide. Several other wells had been dug, one of which supposedly cured a woman of her epilepsy. Actually, the disorder that it cured varies with the tale, but no matter. The well was named Crazy Water and became one of the most famous in town.

Mineral Wells thrived. Celebrities flocked into town, ailing people from across the country came to the small Texas town in droves, and some wells even bottled the water and shipped it to those unfortunates who couldn't visit in person. Because of the amount of traffic, rails were laid into town, and a passenger train began making a regular run in 1891. Things were booming!

In 1920 over 400 mineral water wells had been drilled in the town, and everyone was selling healing water treatments. Bathhouses were constructed, and visitors came not only to drink the therapeutic waters of the town, but also to immerse their bodies in the healing fluid. As you can probably imagine, plans were quickly made for several palatial hotels to house the town's guests. In

1929 Mr. T.B. Baker built his fourteen-story hotel in the middle of town, where it still stands today. It reportedly cost over $1.2 million dollars, had 450 rooms, and one floor that was dedicated solely to the pampering of guests with mineral water baths, massages, and other amenities. A massive swimming pool was constructed at the Baker, one of the largest in the country at the time, and it was filled—of course—with the miraculous healing water of Mineral Wells. The Baker Hotel became a very popular health resort and even a last-ditch effort for people with terminal illnesses. Some moved into the hotel to try to recoup their health, and unfortunately, some died there. There were other famous deaths associated with the hotel, all of which have been sensationalized over the years. A bellboy was crushed by a service elevator and died from the injuries several days later. There have been many stories of shady dealings surrounding his death. In actuality, he was the victim of a tragic accident and nothing more.

The front entrance to the Baker Hotel

On another occasion a woman was found dead in the hotel, and no one had a clue as to who she was. After she was embalmed, the hotel displayed her body in one of the front lobby windows in the hopes that someone would recognize her and provide a clue to her identity—a sight you definitely don't see every day. Just imagine walking down the street of downtown Dallas or Fort Worth and seeing a picture window with a corpse inside. I can only imagine a sign: "Do you know me? Please report inside." I was never able to find out whether anyone identified the poor lady.

One of the final deaths in the hotel was associated with the hotel's namesake. T.B. Baker, the man who built the hotel, died childless in his nineties. He had left the hotel to his nephew, who kept it open as long as he could. When the treatment of disease by mineral water waned among the general public, the nephew closed the hotel in 1963. Local investors purchased it immediately and reopened the hotel in 1964. In 1967 the Baker nephew came to visit and stayed in one of the hotel's best rooms, the Baker Suite. He died there during the night of a heart attack, passing away at the age of seventy-four. The hotel struggled for a few more years and finally closed due to lack of business.

That's how I found the Baker when I made my visit there. Approaching Mineral Wells, it's impossible to miss. You drive into this flat, typical Texas town, and suddenly there's a fourteen-story building rising up from the middle of nowhere. On every other location I visited in the course of writing this book, I relied on street signs and addresses. For the Baker, I just drove into town, saw the building, and headed right for it.

Inside the Baker was very, very strange. The inlaid tile and fine appointments are now in disrepair, but the glamour of its former day was evident. I wondered when supernatural activity started happening, and apparently things had been occurring for some time, because investigative groups have been coming there for years. Baker tour guide Robin Fletcher told me, "The first paranormal group visited here back in the fifties, but a resurgence came just a few years ago."

Shoeshine stand, guest restrooms, and beautiful tile work

Tours are now given by reservation, and if you have at least ten people in your group, you can even schedule an evening tour and spend the night in the grand old hotel. It is listed in the National Register of Historic Places, Building #82004518.

I wondered what had drawn paranormal investigators to this place. As it turns out, strange things started happening in the Baker as soon as it was closed. The first thing people began to notice was that windows would be open at one time, and then when they glanced again, they would be shut. Imagine if you worked across the street from the place, seeing it everyday, and noticed that a particular window was open. But now, think about looking briefly away and then returning your gaze to see that the window was now shut.

This was immediately attributed to the actions of some kind of caretaker or such, but in actuality, the hotel was locked up tight. A caretaker could not be afforded, and when the person who managed the street-level shops retired for the evening, the hotel was completely empty, devoid of all living beings. For whatever reason, though, the windows were opening and lowering themselves at will.

But that was just what was happening during the daytime. During the evening, lights were seen in the rooms of the deserted old hotel. Sometimes it was a full room light, as if a guest had just checked in for the evening, but other times it was a strange, glowing light that could not be explained. In a place that was supposedly deserted, the town's residents often saw a light come on in one room or another, or a single source of light drifting from window to window.

These manifestations take a backseat to the other occurrences at the Baker, however. You see, figures have even been seen standing in a window; yet, no one lives in the hotel! When people walk through the building, there are also scents that are overbearing. The pungent smell of a cigar may waft thorough one hall, while the smell of perfume may be drifting through the next.

A staircase and elevator lobby in the Baker Hotel

Several businesses occupy the ground floor of the Baker, but to really get the feel for the place, contact the group that gives periodic tours and schedule a walk through the grand old hotel. It's hard to look at the surroundings that were once so opulent and plush but now have fallen into disrepair. I felt extremely sad for the place and wished I could have passed through it in the heyday of Mineral Wells. Hobnobbing with the rich and famous, swimming in a pool of healing water, or just looking out across Texas from the top floor, it must have been wonderful. Perhaps that's why a few spirit residents have remained in the old Baker Hotel. Looking at it through eyes that saw it in all its glory might make it hard to leave.

The Baker Hotel
200 E. Hubbard St.
Mineral Wells, TX

# The Ghosts of Rockwall

**W**ell, this chapter is a little different from all of the others. You see, I *really* wanted to find a haunted location in Rockwall, Texas, just to get to write this introductory chapter to the town. There's something there that has absolutely nothing to do with the spirit world but is nevertheless extremely interesting, and I couldn't wait to talk about it: Rockwall's rock wall.

I remember back in the 1960s, I was in the car with my parents and grandparents traveling westward toward Abilene to visit my cousins. As we passed through the city of Rockwall, my grandfather looked over at me and asked, "Sonny boy, do you know why they call this place Rockwall?"

I just shook my head, because I didn't have a clue.

"Because when they were building the city, they found an old rock wall around it, buried in the dirt, that no one could explain."

Turns out that my granddad was absolutely correct; the town was established in 1854, and the residents chose that particular name because of their discovery in 1851 of a stone wall that lay just beneath the surface of the proposed town site.

A nonprofit foundation has been established to study the phenomenon of the buried wall, and you can find out everything about them, and more, at their website www.rockwallfoundation.org. To quote from it, the discovery of the wall happened as follows:

"Of the early settlers, there were three newcomers, T.U. Wade, B.F. Boydston, and a Mr. Stevenson that had arrived to establish a farming community. In 1852 T.U. Wade and his family began building their house on the east side of the east fork of the Trinity River valley near the western edge of the present town site of Rockwall, which is just north of today's Highway 66. In the process of digging the homestead well, Mr. Wade hit a stone formation. Further digging and investigation discovered a rock wall below the surface that ran at an extended length. At the time, Stevenson, Boydston, and Wade were at odds with each other, each wanting to name the town after themselves. On the discovery of the rock wall they decided to name the town Rockwall and resolve their differences. Even though the rock wall at that time had outcroppings around the area that stood two to three feet tall with their capstones in place, no connection had been made to the extent and scope of this fence-like appearance, much less at being an actual wall."

The rock wall itself seems to be rectangular in structure, and although it is buried beneath the surface, the area enclosed by the wall can be extrapolated to measure approximately three and a half miles wide, by approximately five and a half miles long, encompassing almost twenty square miles. Something this structured could hardly be a natural occurrence, which leaves the mystery of who constructed the rock wall?

I realize this is a far cry from any ghosts of North Texas, but it is a very interesting aspect of the town. Could it be that some ancient people had a fortress here? What could possibly explain the mysterious rock wall that exists just outside of the Metroplex?

There's no way to tell for sure, and the folks over at the Rock Wall Foundation are certainly giving it their best effort. It's something I plan on watching, just to see what develops. Mysteries seem to happen in the most unexpected of places!

## The Ghost of One Fast Woman

When I describe Marguerite as a fast woman, I'm certainly not talking about her morals, only the place where she seems to be hanging out. After all, how many ghosts have you heard of that haunt an Indy Racing League team?

The one and only spirit I found in Rockwall is in a rather new building, one made of concrete and metal. It was the home of Team Xtreme Racing for some time, and to be honest, I don't know

Team Xtreme headquarters

exactly who owns the place today. The story of the ghost went on record in *The Dallas Morning News* on June 7, 2000, by a reporter named Dan R. Barber.

Now, Dan Barber is one of the greatest reporters of all time in my humble opinion. I'm basing that, of course, on the fact that he gave me one heckuva great write-up for my last book, *Uncle Bubba's Chicken Wing Fling.* As you can tell, I don't mind a little shameless self-promotion in the least. Honestly, though, Mr. Barber was very sincere but extremely thorough when he interviewed me, so I trust his assessment of the ghost of Marguerite.

Team Xtreme was an open-wheel racing team that ran in the Indy Racing League in the year 2000. I have to say up front that I don't know what's happened to the team, since their web site has been taken down, and they're no longer listed in the Indy Racing League website, but it's possible their team may have been sold or simply moved to another location. The person who may not have made any such move, however, is Marguerite, the spirit that haunts the old Team Xtreme headquarters.

Some of the tricks that she plays on the team are very subtle. An old jukebox, for example, has been known to turn on at full volume on its own. It plays one song then turns right off—something that would be a little uncharacteristic of an electronic anomaly.

The team's crew chief experienced it himself and at first thought someone on the crew might be playing a prank on him. When it happened at two in the morning, when no one else was around, it completely freaked him out. Mr. Lubin told *The Dallas Morning News*, "That one was Garth Brooks' 'If Tomorrow Never Comes.' That's when I grabbed my suitcase and went to the Super 8 Motel down the street."

So many things were happening that the team gave the ghost a name: Marguerite. It may be that the old girl isn't as much of a racecar fan as she is a fixture of the building. At one time the place was a country-western night club called the "Texas Belle" on Interstate 30. That might explain why she seems to like country music so much.

The general manager for the team, John Lopes, told *The Dallas Morning News*, "It's kind of fun to have a ghost around. It's a friendly ghost so far."

Strange voices have also been heard around the shop, so it is even possible that Marguerite isn't there alone, although she is the only ghost that has actually been seen. Lillie O'Brien, the team's administrative assistant, was working out one day in the team exercise room when she caught a glimpse of a woman sitting behind her. She was walking on the treadmill at the time and saw a reflection of someone just sitting there. Ms. O'Brien said, "When I turned to look, there was nothing there. But I saw the reflection in the glass." The spirit had been sitting on the weight bench about fifteen feet away.

So how did the name Marguerite come up? Well, although everyone knew about the ghost, no one had given her a name. When the team had a Christmas party at the shop and the subject of the spirit came up, everyone was having a margarita—the name Marguerite just stuck.

According to Ms. O'Brien, the ghost is a young lady with black hair and pale skin. There's no indication as to why she has chosen to stay at the old Texas Belle building, but apparently she is really there—at least for the time being.

Although something may have happened to the racing team (and I couldn't get any response from them), I was able to locate a Rockwall native who remembered the Texas Belle very well.

"It was kind of a community honky-tonk. You'd go there and see your friends, your boss, your co-workers, all having a great time." When I asked about the ghost, however, he didn't have a clue. "I never saw anything that looked like a ghost there. Maybe the people who owned the place would have something to say about it, but for us, it was just a place to have a beer and get a dance or two if we were lucky."

So, as they say in court, I cannot confirm or deny the presence of Marguerite. All I do know is there are a few people who firmly believe.

Team Xtreme
Interstate 30
Rockwall, TX

# The Ghosts of Waxahachie

In case you're keeping score, Waxahachie is yet another county seat, established in 1850 in Ellis County, and the last one we'll be visiting in North Texas. The city's name comes from an Indian word that means cow, or buffalo, and is also the name of a local creek where such animals watered many years ago.

Five gentlemen were the first settlers in the community and were the founders of the city: Emory W. Rogers, J. D. Templeton, W. H. Getzendaner, B. F. Hawkins, and J. H. Spalding. A courthouse was erected in 1850 to accompany the other businesses that had sprung up in town, including a general store and a post office. Churches soon followed, and just before the Civil War started, there were already five located there.

Waxahachie officially incorporated in 1871, and a railroad line was constructed for the trade of cotton and lumber with neighboring communities. The railroad continued to expand its reach outward, and by the 1920s businesses in town numbered over two hundred, and included banks, cotton gins, textile mills, cottonseed oil mills, a newspaper, a broom factory, a clothing factory, and even an ice cream factory.

The city has enjoyed a steady growth over the years, but in the last few decades it has taken a role as a destination for tourists looking for a place to escape. Its annual Scarborough Faire Renaissance Festival and Screams Halloween Park attract visitors by the thousands, and Waxahachie has acquired the nickname "The Gingerbread City" because of the beautiful architecture of the historical homes and buildings located there. A Gingerbread Trail is a yearly event in the city that showcases Victorian-style houses with gingerbread carpentry, the most popular architectural style, as well as combinations with Queen Ann, Classic Renaissance, or Roman Doric revival architecture. A Christmas tour of homes is also presented every December to highlight some of the homes in town decorated for the season.

Waxahachie's charm and old world atmosphere have made it a wonderful getaway for a few hours to shop and dine, or an entire weekend at one of its charming bed and breakfasts, some of which are in this book. The small-town atmosphere has also drawn Hollywood's eye, and the city has been used as a location for several movies that you've probably seen: *Tender Mercies*, *Places in the Heart*, and *The Trip to Bountiful*.

The city was a place I was very familiar with long before I started writing this book. I've been on many of the home tours, enjoyed Scarborough Faire, and enjoyed many meals at the Catfish Plantation. Since I knew the latter was notoriously haunted, I figured from the very start of this book that I'd be visiting Waxahachie in my travels.

What I found, though, was that there were several places in town that had a few ghostly tales. Most of them were bed and breakfasts, places the city is famous for, and also a remote location called "Becky Road."

Because of the lack of supporting evidence or even a story to go by, I had to leave the Becky Road Ghost out of the book. The miniscule information I did find was that Private John Hemerich's ghost has been seen standing on the side of the road. The private is rumored to be the last Confederate hanged by the Union army, but I couldn't find anything to substantiate even that fact. Since there was also a lack of anyone who'd actually seen the ghost, I just didn't have enough information for a story. If you're driving down Becky Road, though, and see a Confederate apparition there, please let me know! I'd love to put it in a future book.

Meanwhile, on to a few places in town that definitely have a ghost story or two to tell.

# The Motherly Ghost of the Bonnynook Inn

The Bonnynook Inn is located on one of the main drags in Waxahachie, but when you step into the protection of the small grove of trees surrounding it, you've passed into a calmer, simpler world. I visited there on a warm Wednesday afternoon, and as I sat on the front porch waiting for Mr. Franks, I think I could have stayed in that chair forever. The air seemed cooler, calmer, and the birds in the trees had an extremely relaxing song that, if I'd had a tall glass of iced tea, I could have listened to all day.

The Bonnynook feels like a world away from the hustle and bustle of the work world, something I think the innkeepers planned and continue to carefully nurture. Mr. Franks and I sat out on the front porch and had a wonderful visit, while he told me about the history of the bed and breakfast. Of course, my first question was about the ghosts.

He just smiled and said, "Oh, we've got a few things that happen occasionally. They used to be a lot more frequent, but they've calmed down in the last few years." All the activity seemed to center around a room in the upstairs of their Inn that they named the Morrow Room and a tragic tale that went along with the house.

The Sitting Room of the Bonnynook Inn

Originally, the place was constructed on speculation by a builder, which was a little unusual for the day. At the time, Waxahachie was a cotton and railroad boomtown, and he knew that as people moved into the town, he would be able to sell the house to a family with means enough to buy the two-story home.

Sure enough, in 1887 a doctor and his family came into town in search of a place to live. The wife fell in love with the place, and so Dr. West made the necessary arrangements to purchase the house. He and his wife moved in, along with his sister-in-law. It wasn't long before the couple was blessed with a son, and the family was extremely happy in their new home.

The only difference in the configuration of the house then was that the kitchen was external to the structure, a common practice in those days. Kitchens were places where fire was used abundantly, and should it catch fire—God forbid—then the house would not be harmed.

In 1895, however, the house was "modernized" and the kitchen was moved inside the home—something that would play a heartbreaking role in the history of the West family. A new wood-burning stove was added to the kitchen in 1896, an elaborate model for most families. Along with all the cooking surfaces and baking chambers, there was a container in one side of the stove that could be filled with water. As the fire heated the stove for cooking, it would also boil the water so the family could have warm baths, hot water to wash dishes, and so forth. The West family must have felt they were truly living in the lap of luxury.

As Mr. Franks was telling me the wonderful tale of the Wests on the front porch, I knew there had to be a sad twist coming, and sure enough, there was. There was an explosion in the kitchen one day, and Mr. Franks could only speculate that something heavy had been set on the top of the water chamber, allowing the steam to build up more and more pressure. When it blew, Mrs. West was standing right there and was killed by the forceful blast as the stove ripped apart.

A funeral was held, the family mourned, and a few eyebrows were raised when, just three months after the tragic accident, Dr. West married his wife's sister.

It may have simply been a marriage of convenience, since there was still a small boy to raise, and the sister had been there since his birth. Or perhaps it was the case where Dr. West just couldn't bear to be alone, nor would it be proper for the woman and him to live in the house together now that his wife had died. No matter what, life slowly went on, and the tale of the West family ends there. Sort of.

The house changed hands a few times, but for the most part, time passed without incident. In 1983 the house was up for sale again, and Mr. and Mrs. Franks found the old home, immediately knowing that it would make a beautiful bed and breakfast.

As they walked through the house, the couple was told that the upstairs had not been occupied for thirty years, and there was one particular room that was locked around 1910, and the door had not been opened since.

I couldn't help but smile as Mr. Franks was telling me about the room, since the story had all the makings of a classic Hollywood scary movie! A room that had been locked for some mysterious reason, where no human had set foot inside for some seventy-odd years—it was the kind of thing you could only find in theaters. I think that may be one of the problems people have when they start talking about ghosts, though. Visions of movies such as *Poltergeist* and *The Amityville Horror* jump into our heads, when in reality, I've never heard of any presence like that occupying a building. Most spirits are benevolent, maybe a little sad, or perhaps a bit mischievous.

I asked Mr. Franks what they did when they heard about the locked room, and he just smiled and said, "We unlocked it!" They found exactly what you would expect from a place that had been closed up for so long: some water damage, mildew here and there, basically a room that was badly in need of repair.

And repair it they did. The Morrow Room, as it is now known, is one of the most beautiful in the bed and breakfast. But as guests started staying in the room, especially in the first few years, a few strange things were reported when they came downstairs for breakfast.

Faint voices were occasionally heard in the room, although the guests couldn't quite determine what was being said. A few times a faint image could be seen in the room, which didn't bother anyone but would just fade in and out. One of the most interesting things that happened was the singing of lullabies in the Morrow Room. They were soft, melodic, soothing, but in a foreign tongue that the guests couldn't seem to place.

One family that stayed in the room had a Czechoslovakian background, though, and recognized the words as being from an old Czech song that mothers would sing to their babies.

The Morrow Room, site of the interesting activity at the Bonnynook

Mr. Franks told me he believes the room originally belonged to the sister-in-law, but that the spirit of the wife seemed to be the one visiting it. Perhaps when her sister moved into her husband's room, she took it over so she could still be around her family. Mrs. West may have wanted to be there to sing an occasional lullaby to her son. Since many people with Czech origins moved into the area around the same time as the West family, it is possible Mrs. West had that background and was simply singing the songs she remembered from her own mother.

In any case, the supernatural activity has slowed down in the Morrow Room, and few guests come downstairs with questions and tales anymore. It is a lovely room, though, and I paused there during my tour of the Inn, listening carefully, hoping to hear a few faint strains of a tune, accompanied by the soft sounds of a mother's voice. When I return to the Bonnynook, this will definitely be the room I ask for. After all, if something like that did happen, could there possibly be a better way to fall asleep?

Bonnynook Inn
414 West Main Street
Waxahachie, TX 75165
Phone: 972.938.7207
Toll Free: 800.486.5936
Web: http://www.bonnynook.com

## The Family Spirits of the Rose of Sharon

If you happen to be a gardener, then you might hear the term
"Rose of Sharon" and think about a beautiful garden bush with a
white flower and a crimson center. On the other hand, someone
skilled in the quilting arts might picture a block pattern that's
moderately hard to complete but makes a beautiful quilt.

There was something completely different in Sharon Shawn's mind, though, when she first laid eyes on the old house on Bryson Street in Waxahachie.

As the story goes, in 1892 an attorney named F.P. Powell moved to Waxahachie to practice law and built a lovely two-story home for him and his wife. Over the next twenty years, the couple had a wonderful life in the small Texas town, and two little girls were born to them during that time, right there in the house on Bryson Street.

F.P. Powell will always be remembered in Waxahachie history because in July of 1896, he sold a plot of land on Wyatt Street to the Waxahachie Independent School District for $500. This land was used to build the Oak Lawn School, one of the first African-American schools in Waxahachie during those times of segregation in Texas. Soon after the land was purchased, the first class was graduated from Oak Lawn High School: two young men and two young ladies. The gentlemen were Prince Goldthwaite and Robert Davis, both of whom attended college and then returned to their hometown of Waxahachie to become principals of the school.

The Powell family's time in Waxahachie would come to an end in 1912, when F.P. Powell received an offer from a firm in Austin that he simply couldn't afford to pass up. Reluctantly, the family packed all of their belongings and left the town and the house that they loved so much.

The place changed hands several times in the next three decades and slowly slipped into disrepair here and there. The owners simply didn't have the passion for the place that the Powells did.

An owner that purchased the house in the late to mid-1940s took an extremely drastic step. The lovely wrap-around porches on both floors were enclosed and made into several small rooms. This allowed the owner to use it as a boardinghouse, squeezing as many people in as possible. The house existed in this manner for another three decades.

The house was sold again in the seventies, this time to a single-parent family. They struggled to keep payments up for about ten years, but unfortunately, the house was repossessed in 1987. The majestic old beauty stood vacant for about four years, fell further into cosmetic disrepair, and became tangled in vines and wild growth.

Some say that a house with a soul waits for the perfect owner to come along, holding out for that one special person to love it. This may have been the case with Sharon Shawn and her husband, because even though the place was overgrown with vegetation and the porches had been enclosed and hidden from the outside world, there was a magic between the couple and the old place.

Inspectors were called in to give their blessing on the purchase, and when the foundation and basic construction of the house were found to be sound, the final papers were signed.

Ms. Shawn may have been given the first indication that the house was happy with her when she visited it before the workmen had even begun the restoration process. Wanting to take a look around her new place, she set her purse down in the middle of the floor of the room that would eventually become the dining room in the finished home. She explored the house at length, stopping to sift through some newspapers and magazines that were in one of the back rooms. She was enjoying herself so much that the time got away, and it was getting late before she knew it.

Knowing that she had to get back to her current house, she went back to retrieve her purse, but there was something not far from it that wasn't there before: a pair of 14 karat gold earrings. And not just any earrings; these were a set that Sharon had lost a year ago, long before she had ever laid eyes on the Powell house.

There was no rational explanation as to how the earrings could have come to be in that room, and they were obviously placed near her purse so she would see them. Perhaps the Powells were letting Ms. Shawn know that they approved of her as the new owner for the house they'd loved so much. In any case, the earrings were a mystery—but not the last one she would experience there.

The room that is believed to be the Powell master bedroom is now a guestroom at the bed and breakfast. Several times Sharon has seen a family of four in the bathroom area, standing formally together as if posing for some spectral portrait. There is a father in a gray suit and top hat, a woman wearing a long dress in 1800s style, and two little girls. Both of the children are in white dresses with sashes, but one has a doll in her arms. Although it has only rarely happened, it is not a frightful occurrence, only a startling one.

A presence is sometimes felt in that room: a warm, pleasant sensation of some loving soul who is there. Other manifestations occur more frequently but are much less dramatic: the sounds of music softly drifting through the house, footsteps in the hallway when no guests are there, and the creaking of steps on an empty stairway, as if someone was walking up them. These things don't frighten the guests or the innkeepers, and if I were Ms. Shawn, they wouldn't bother me, either. After all, any spirits that might be in the house made one fact abundantly clear some time ago: *You are welcome here!*

Rose of Sharon
205 Bryson Street
Waxahachie, TX 75165
972.938.8833

# The Strange Caller of the Chaska House

"Victorian Splendor." If you trust *Texas Highways Magazine* at all—and Lord knows that I do, since as much as I love to travel around Texas, their magazine is a constant source of inspiration for me—then you'll have to take their simple yet profound description of the place to heart.

Before visiting the Chaska House, I swapped several emails with Louis Brown, who now owns the bed and breakfast with his wife, Linda. To be honest, it was hard to get a time to visit, because

they were always booked. That's a better testament to the quality of their inn than anything I could possibly write.

If you visit their web page, you'll find that they describe themselves by saying, "The Chaska House celebrates the joyous revival style and attitude that flourished in turn-of-the-century Waxahachie. National Register-listed, the Chaska House (c. 1900) features an extensive collection of period antiques assembled over many years by your hosts. Guests may enjoy the fascinating library, grand hall, formal dining room, bustling kitchen, wrap-around veranda, and tree-shaded grounds. All just a short stroll to the town square with its wondrous shops, excellent restaurants, and magnificent courthouse that James Michener called 'a fairytale palace—one of the finest buildings in Texas.' Guest rooms are romantic, tall and spacious with sitting areas and private baths. A full southern breakfast will satisfy any appetite."

There was an old television show where the tag-line for the star was, "No brag, just fact," and that seems to suit the Chaska House's self-description perfectly. The spirits of this place have manifested themselves in a particularly interesting manner.

The house was originally built in 1900 by Edward and Marie Chaska. Edward was a businessman who owned a dry goods store on the square in Waxahachie. Today the town square has antique stores where visitors can peruse all kinds of goodies, but back then it was the center of commerce—the perfect place for Mr. Chaska to peddle all kinds of things including baking flour, textiles, millenary, and even number two wash tubs.

In an unfortunate twist of fate for the Chaskas, Edward took ill and was away seeking specialized medical treatment when he died at the young age of fifty-three years old.

I have to stop and say that, yes, fifty-three is young. I remember being in junior high school and thinking that eighteen was really, really old, but at my present age, fifty looks very young indeed. In any case, Mr. Chaska passed away. His wife Marie kept the house and continued to live there until her death in 1953. To say the least, it was an interesting coincidence that Mr. Chaska died at the age of fifty-three, and Mrs. Chaska died in 1953.

But no matter, the story continues on. Edward and Marie had no children of their own, and since Marie had never prepared a will, their home was sold at auction on the courthouse steps in 1953. Now, if you've never heard of the phrase "on the courthouse steps," that is the way many of these real estate get-rich-quick programs advise people to pick up property. That wasn't the case here, though, because the house was bought by a couple, J.F. and O.B. Dunaway, as a residence.

They then sold the property to James and Ruth Saxon, who lived in it together until they both died, within two years of each other.

The next occupant was Miss Sadie Ralston, who had married a man named Mr. A.L. Hardesty. Miss Ralston—or Mrs. Hardesty, as the case was—taught school in Waxahachie in 1968. When the house was sold next, it went to the hands of a family named Fuller, then the McBurneys, and finally to the hands of Louis and Linda Brown, who purchased the house in 1980 and began the task of restoring it to its original beauty.

As part of the restoration, and in preparation for its new life as a bed and breakfast, the old telephone system in the house was replaced with a new one with all the latest features. The Browns were having a quiet dinner one evening soon after that, when they heard the sound of a telephone ringing. It wasn't the phone nearest to the dining table, and when they couldn't find the phone anywhere in the vicinity, they launched a full-scale search for the source. The ringing was finally traced to one of the older telephones that had been replaced but not removed from the house. It was in a box with other phones and was disconnected from the new telephone system. Louis and the rest of the family just looked from the phone, to each other, then to the phone, and back again.

Finally, Louis picked up the telephone and said a cautious, "Hello?"

He heard what sounded like the voice of a proper lady, who said, "May I speak to Mrs. Curline?" Almost in shock, Louis told the mysterious caller she had the wrong number. He then hung up the receiver of the phone, and being a curious kind of fellow, he picked it back up to see what was going on. There was only a dead, disconnected silence from the receiver. The telephone was not working.

It was a curious enough event that he just had to ask around, and Louis found out that a Mrs. Curline had lived across the street many years ago but had been deceased for some time. This is the perfect example of a situation where additional information makes an odd case even more interesting. It's hard to imagine why the old telephone system would be the focus of some otherworldly activity, yet at the Chaska house, that was the case. Whether it was a welcome to their new home, or just a reminder that they were only the latest owners in a historical line, it made an impression on Louis Brown, and it's one of his favorite stories to tell.

While you probably won't receive any phantom phone calls at the Chaska House, it is a wonderful place to stay in Waxahachie. All it takes is a casual stroll over to the town square and you can enjoy a museum, antique shopping, and wonderful restaurants. For an extra exposure to ghosts, you might even stop by the Catfish Plantation just down the street.

Whatever the case, though, as I visit the Chaska House, I'll always get goose bumps when I hear the telephone in my room ring. One never knows who might be calling.

Chaska House
716 West Main Street
Waxahachie, TX 75165
Phone: 972.937.3390
Toll Free: 800.931.3390
Email: chaskabb@azmail.net

# The Phantom Trio of the Catfish Plantation

Fried catfish is almost a religion to me. I'm not quite ready to call myself a connoisseur, but I've probably eaten enough catfish in my life to fill a reasonable-sized lake. For that reason, I have a personal affinity for the last place that I scheduled for this book, the Catfish Plantation. This restaurant serves up some of the best catfish you'll ever put in your mouth. And their hushpuppies, well, don't even get me started—not if you want to hear about the ghosts, that is.

Just a few blocks from downtown Waxahachie is a Victorian farmhouse that was built over a century ago. Although a neighborhood has now grown up around it, the structure still retains an air of elegance in its old age.

A farmer named Anderson built the house in 1895, and it became the residence of several families over the years until 1970, when it was converted to a doctor's office.

Following that, a few unsuccessful restaurants occupied the house, but it finally found a niche as the "Catfish Plantation." The restaurant was established on the premise of wonderful food featuring fried, blackened, or baked catfish. The hushpuppies receive rave reviews, and visitors love the green beans and other side dishes. I can personally vouch for it all!

As the folks at the restaurant started serving up this delectable cuisine, however, odd things began to be noticed by both the staff and patrons. Objects moved around by themselves, mysterious noises were heard, and visitors reported strange phenomenon.

I had the opportunity to visit with Jimmy Poarch, the restaurant's owner, who was kind enough to acquaint me with the spirits inhabiting the Catfish Plantation.

One of them is a gentleman farmer named Will, who is said to have died in the house back in the 1930s. Will's favorite area seems to be the old front porch, which has been enclosed as an entryway and waiting area for the restaurant.

Another of the ghosts, Caroline, is said to be displeased with the strangers who are constantly visiting her house. It is thought that Caroline is a woman who lived in the house from the 1950s until 1970. Psychics that have visited the Catfish Plantation say that even though she passed away at the age of eighty, she doesn't realize she has died. Caroline is most active in the kitchen of the restaurant, although she has been known to wander through the dining rooms to interact with the guests.

The front porch, now an entryway, which is Will's favorite haunt

The third presence is that of Elizabeth Anderson, the daughter of the farmer who built the house. Mr. Poarch related the tragic tale of Elizabeth to me during our visit: It was her wedding day and should have been the happiest time of her life. She was dressed in her gown and veil and was ready to go to the church where everyone awaited her entrance. A former boyfriend came to the house and told Elizabeth that her father had sent him to bring her to the wedding ceremony. As the bride-to-be went back to her bedroom to retrieve a few articles before leaving, the man followed her back then strangled her right there in the bedroom, an area that is now the restrooms for the Catfish Plantation. Elizabeth's presence can be detected as a cold spot in the room or a gentle whiff of the fragrant scent of roses.

Some people report seeing the figures of the ghosts in the restaurant: Elizabeth in the front bay windows, and Will out on the porch. Although he's never seen one of the ghosts himself, Mr. Poarch has no doubt that they exist in his restaurant. "The most common thing that happens is when I'm in the restaurant and no one else is around, I'll feel the presence of someone standing right behind me. I turn around and there's nobody there. That happens a lot."

One of the most startling encounters he's had with the spirits happened one evening at about eleven o'clock. Mr. Poarch was giving a private tour of the restaurant for a celebrity who was in town and was entering the restroom area, which used to be the young bride-to-be's bedroom. There is one door on an automatic closer that leads to a small hall, and from there you can enter the ladies' or gentlemen's restroom, whichever is appropriate. The small group had gone past the first door, which had already closed, and stopped for Mr. Poarch to relate the story of the strangled bride. As he was doing so, the first door opened up, of its own accord, and then closed again.

Another evening, Mr. Poarch was entertaining at a private party after the restaurant had closed. In one of the dining rooms there, a tray of silverware that had just been washed was on a side table out of the way of the guests. The tray suddenly started to shake, rattling the silverware with loud metallic clanks. No one was near the tray, and everyone just sat and watched, until it finally stopped.

It's hard to determine which spirit is causing a disturbance at any given time, and in fact, the wait staff all have their individual accounts of things happening at the Catfish Plantation. When things are busy during peak hours, most supernatural activity goes unnoticed. When things slow down, however, the ghosts make their presence known. The most common are extreme cold and hot spots, especially in the area of the ladies' restroom. Silverware has also been knocked off the table as if someone had just walked by and accidentally bumped it off, but of course, no one is around.

Caroline was raised a staunch Baptist, and her spirit still disapproves of alcohol in her house. While the restaurant does not serve beer or wine, patrons sometimes bring in their own to accompany a meal. A glass of wine is sometimes knocked off of the table, as Caroline passes though and shows her displeasure.

One of the dining rooms frequented by Caroline

There are enough stories about the Catfish Plantation to go on for hours, so it is probably easier to say that it is one of the most supernaturally active places in North Texas, and it is well worth a trip to Waxahachie.

The Catfish Plantation is open Thursday through Sunday and is available for private parties on the other weekdays. Myself, I've long made it a point to stop in for a meal anytime I'm passing through town. The food is a rare treat, and there's always the chance of running into one of the ghosts—the phantom trio of Will, Caroline, and Elizabeth are certainly active participants in the day-to-day activities of the restaurant. When you visit, take a few minutes to read through the notebooks of experiences written by the guests. There are several volumes, each one a testament to the ghostly goings-on there. Incredible things have happened to the patrons of the restaurant, and I don't just mean the wonderful catfish and hushpuppies that are served there. Be prepared to encounter a cold spot in the ladies' restroom, have your place setting moved around on the table in front of you, or even sense a presence standing near as you dine on your meal. If you bring along a bottle of wine, though, keep an eye out for Caroline. She may pay a personal visit to your table, just to keep you in line!

The Catfish Plantation
814 Water Street at Gibson Street
Waxahachie, TX 75165
Phone: 972.937.9468

# A Few Words in Closing

**W**ell, there they are—the ghosts of North Texas. If you've had as good a time reading this book as I did writing it, then I feel like I've done my job. It's been one heckuva great journey.

Putting this book together has been an interesting six months. I've traveled all over North Texas, made more telephone calls than I can remember, sent even more emails, and talked to many, many wonderful people. I think the individuals who shared their stories with me were the best part of it all. And of course, I visited all of these places myself. One week I put over a thousand miles on my car. But it was fun…a *lot* of fun! My hope is that you will enjoy checking out some of these locations just as much as I did.

Whether you live in North Texas and are using this book as a travel guide for a weekend getaway, or you're from out of the area and want to check out some of the haunted locations on an upcoming visit, you'll find that all of these places are worth your time.

Ghost hunting or not, you won't find a better meal than the delicious entrees at the Catfish Plantation, burgers and cheese fries at Snuffer's on Greenville Avenue, or one of the mouthwatering cuts of beef at Del Frisco's Double Eagle Steak House. The places to stay that we've visited in the book all have their own unique elegance and charm, whether you're sitting out on the front porch of one of the North Texas bed and breakfasts, soaking in the history of the Old West at the Stockyards Hotel, or in a plush room overlooking downtown Dallas at the historic old Adolphus.

While you're out and about, be sure to catch a live performance at one of the theaters I found: the Majestic, the Farr Best, or the Granbury Opera House. Dance the night away at the Lizard Lounge, or hear live music and enjoy a cold one at the historic old Sons of Hermann Hall; the people there are just plain friendly. No

**217**

matter which direction you go, I think you'll have a great time. I sure did.

Not that every haunted location in North Texas is in this book. There were some folks I contacted who didn't want to be included, afraid if it came out that their place had a ghost story or two, it might be bad for business. A few others felt like the idea of ghosts and such are evil, and they didn't want to have any part of it at all. That was very odd to me, since not a single place I visited had anything that was remotely frightening, or had any bad feelings associated with the spirits there. They all seemed very kind and gentle, and some were downright mischievous and fun! Evil? Naw, no way.

I also know I've missed a few places because I just didn't know about them. My biggest disappointment is going to be when I'm at a book signing or some other promotional appearance, and someone comes up to me and says, "Why didn't you put my business in the book—we have a ghost!" The fact is, I've included everything here that I could find and visit on my own. If you know of other places, I'd love to hear about them. My email is at the bottom of this chapter.

While you're out on your travels, I hope you won't spend too much time looking for ghosts at Smiley's Grave or Screaming Bridge. And while White Rock Lake is certainly a beautiful place to visit, you're simply not going to find the Lady of the Lake there, no matter how many books she's been written up in. The old girl is an urban legend—albeit an entertaining one—but nothing more.

Looking at the ghosts that are very real, however, some of the most interesting things I found in researching this book are the different types of manifestations that people encounter. Just stop and think how varied some of them are:

✧ The presence at the Texas White House, who can be felt lying down on the bed beside a guest, yet is not there when the light is turned on. The same phenomenon has occurred at the Tarlton House, if you remember.

- A figure that appears as much human as you or I, but simply vanishes, as is the case with the young lady at the Baroness Inn, or the man in the black suit at the Jett Building.
- The sound of music in the air that occurs at the Tarlton House, Adolphus Hotel, or the Bonnynook Inn when no earthly music is playing.
- Disturbances with electric lights or other objects, as the actors and staff of the Granbury Opera House or the Farr Best Theater have observed.
- Sudden odors in the air, like the lilac blossoms at Log Cabin Village, roses at the Catfish Plantation, or citrus at the Wright Place.
- And phantom footsteps in empty rooms and hallways; this most common of occurrences seems to happen *everywhere*!

Why do spirits have *so many different* ways of interacting with us? I couldn't tell you; and perhaps if I had some kind of inkling, it would take some of the mystery away from them.

The truth is, no one knows for sure what these spirits are, why they still seem to be showing up in our world, or what business they may still have here.

Some people conjecture that there isn't any conscious thought associated with them, that they're just impressions of a bygone era. That doesn't explain why the table settings of Snuffer's Restaurant are inexplicably moved around by unseen hands, though; the building wasn't configured in the same way, if it had tables at all, before Pat Snuffer acquired the place and turned it into a Mecca for cheese-fries.

And what about the phantom elevator operator at the Sammons Center for the Arts? If the spirit of a young man still resides there, it would certainly explain why he opens the door when a pretty, young girl walks by. All I know is that when I was there, he certainly didn't do me the courtesy!

On the other hand, the apparition of Mr. Tarlton on the third floor of Tarlton House or the young lady giving instructions on the proper way to dress to patrons of the Baroness Inn seem to fit the description perfectly of someone who is simply still repeating actions from their time on Earth.

Much better minds than mine have contemplated such questions about the unknown through the ages, though, and it is therefore doubtful I will resolve the issue here. Many religions speak out against even questioning the things of this nature that happen all around us, perhaps because it is impossible for mere mortals to understand them.

I do know one thing for certain: these things exist. I have seen apparitions with my own eyes, I've followed a cloud of heavy floral perfume around the hallway of a hotel for several hours, I've heard footsteps walking across the floor of an empty room and walked into a mass of something that I can only describe as "heavy air" or an energy field of some type that put me in sensory overload. All these, and much more, have actually happened to me. But even if I wasn't to be believed, there are the experiences of all the people I met in the course of writing this book, and they can't all be wrong.

Examine the evidence, and you'll have to acknowledge that in each of these places, something is there, and in many, many different ways, we are being made aware of their presence.

If it is impossible for us to determine exactly what it is or who they are and what they are still doing here, then my advice is simple: seek out what experiences you can find and enjoy them! In many ways, the fun is in putting the pieces of the puzzle together, not having it solved. Speaking of which, some folks work for many hours on a jigsaw puzzle and when they're done, laminate it and hang it on the wall as proof of their conquest. Not me. If I ever get a puzzle together, I immediately tear it apart and start another one. The entertainment is in the journey, not the destination.

And so I'll close out this book. As I write these last words, I'm sitting at a desk in a notoriously haunted room where a particular ghost has been experienced by many people. After the final word is typed, I'm just going to shut down my computer, turn off the light, sit here for a few minutes, and see if anyone shows up. If so, maybe I'll ask them about the nature of ghosts, but if not, it's a lot of fun just to be here. What better way to finish this book than in the presence of the supernatural.

Until we meet again,

Mitchel Whitington
mitchel@whitington.com

# Index

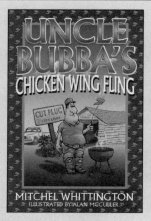

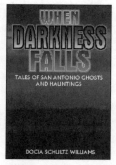